BILL

C90 3982

D1098839

# Fool's Gold

Trouble struck with the powerful boom from a large caliber rifle, the sound quickly evaporating like a rare morning mist in the hot desert air. The Whip felt the passing of the heavy slug as it blasted a hole in his hat and then tore off some wood molding on the back of the stagecoach before kicking up dust in the road. Whoever was shooting had just barely missed him, and the Whip knew he was in serious trouble. He leaned over, creating a smaller profile, and began yelling and snapping the reins on the rumps of his four-horse team in a desperate attempt to increase their pace.

# Fool's Gold

Eric Niven

A Black Horse Western

ROBERT HALE

© Eric Niven 2020
First published in Great Britain in 2020

ISBN 978-0-7198-3127-0

The Crowood Press
The Stable Block
Crowood Lane
Ramsbury
Marlborough
Wiltshire SN8 2HR

www.bhwesterns.com

Robert Hale is an imprint
of The Crowood Press

The right of Eric Niven to be identified as
author of this work has been asserted by him
in accordance with the Copyright, Designs
and Patents Act 1988

*To Errol, named after another good man, and Elise, a silent support.*
*My special thanks to Cathi, Jim, and Stacey*

Typeset by
Simon and Sons ITES Services Pvt Ltd
Printed and bound in Great Britain by
4Bind Ltd, Stevenage, SG1 2XT

# PROLOGUE

It was like any day in beautiful Virginia, only a looming fog of uncertainty marred the serenity. Richmond, Virginia, the current capital of the Confederate States of America, was bathed in humidity and brilliant sunshine, with just enough of a breeze to roll the national flag. Adopted 1 May 1863, the Stainless Banner, the second national flag of the Confederate States of America, stood proudly against the brilliant blue sky as Colonel Franks saluted it and walked into the White House of the Confederacy.

Passing approved through three doors flanked by teamed sentries and ignored by busy civilians at desks, Colonel Franks finally arrived at his destination. The lone sentry saluted and opened the door to allow Colonel Franks into the room that contained the financial inner workings of the Confederacy. Three men in formal attire were seated around a heavy table spread with stacks of official documents and various papers. It was obvious that the meeting in progress was tense, as all three men were perspiring – and not just from the heat and humidity.

Ignoring the Colonel's entrance, the three men continued to argue back and forth over possible sources of revenue. The Union blockade of Southern ports was strangling the life of the Southern economy and the war effort. The anemic Confederate government was being compelled to issue bonds and print money to stave off economic collapse.

'We have the market and the raw materials,' said the wasted-looking slim man, who looked as anemic as the economy he was trying to revive. 'If we could just break the blockade we could sell our cotton!'

'We have blockade runners!' offered the shaggy white-haired man, who seemed to be conducting the meeting but was now just trying to restore calm.

'We just can't depend on blockade runners to pro-vide all the supplies we so desperately need,' shouted the rotund man in response.

'Yes, yes, we have gone over this *ad nauseam*, Josiah.'

'Colonel Franks reporting as ordered,' Colonel Franks said, deciding he should announce himself while keeping the stiff bearing of the military so evident in his very being.

'Yes, thank you, Colonel,' the man with the shaggy white hair said over his shoulder before turning back to the other two seated men. 'Obviously this discussion needs further attention, and I appreciate your insights and comments, but rest assured we have plans for breaking the blockade and even for finding additional sources of revenue.'

'Are you referring to the iron clad *Virginia*, which is nearing completion, or the drawing-board torpedo boats?' the rotund man said sarcastically, mopping his sweating bald head with a white handkerchief.

'Yes, those are two of our efforts,' the white-haired man said calmly, ignoring the negativity of the previous question.

'And the sources of additional revenue?' the sickly looking man asked.

'To be shared at the proper time, gentlemen,' the white-haired man announced as he stood up, signaling the end of the meeting. 'Now if you will excuse me, the patient Colonel and I have some business to attend to. We will meet again tomorrow.'

Calmly escorting his two unsatisfied and disgruntled visitors to the door, the white-haired man turned to the guard without and said, 'Sergeant, see that we are not disturbed.'

'Yes, sir,' came the practiced reply.

The white-haired man carefully and quietly closed the door and turned back to the rigid Colonel. After walking around to again face the Colonel and then motioning to one of the now vacant seats, he said, 'Can I get you anything to drink, Colonel?'

'No, sir, but thank you for offering,' Franks responded, a little on edge as he made his way to the closest chair and sat down, wondering what was next. He had an inkling regarding his invitation here, but he was, as always, overly cautious.

Seeing the rigid bearing, far beyond the normal military training of his obviously uncomfortable guest, the white-haired man decided to get right to the point of their meeting. 'So Colonel, your plan...' he hesitated, '...is being implemented. I still have my doubts, which explains the secrecy of this operation and my precautions about this meeting, but I wanted you to know the item is on its way. I am not as confident in the courier as are those who hired him, so I have taken additional precautions. But since this is your idea, I wanted you to know the specifics of the operation...'

# ONE

Out west, the dust just is. It blankets everything. Dust, the smell of horses, and the unwashed. The atmosphere of the Concord stagecoach, midway in this fifty-mile leg of its journey, was typical. Four travelers, three men and one woman, all heading west for personal reasons.

Rory Sean MacTavish sat slouched on his side of the red leather bench with his hat pulled down over his eyes, his body accepting every pitch and roll of the ride. He was used to rough ride and the dust and the smell of the other two male travelers, but the woman was not. She kept putting toilet water around her as an olfactory defense, but because her dainty red lace handkerchief seemed permanently attached to her nose, Rory could tell she was losing the battle.

Smalltalk at this point of the trek was non-existent. The weary travelers had reached the point of exhaustion when only endurance mattered. The new and expanding railroad could only take them so far, so from Salt Lake City, a stagecoach was required. This leg of their journey went through hot, monotonous desert, rattle and bump. Time seemed only measured by the number of telegraph poles they passed. Unbeknownst to these weary travelers and the Whip, who kept a strong hold on the horses' reins, their arrival had been anticipated and now they were being carefully watched.

A cool, experienced and callused hand balanced a Sharps buffalo gun on a small sandbag, brought along to ensure stability for long distance shooting. Lying next to the sandbag stood two carefully positioned cartridges, lined up for quick retrieval should the first shot miss. The breach of the heavy rifle had already been opened and one 45-70 cartridge had been inserted and the breach closed. The set trigger was pulled and the hunter was now simply waiting for the stagecoach to reach the predetermined position. Sighting through the peepsight, the hunter watched as the seconds passed and the stagecoach drew closer. One hundred and fifty yards was estimated. Quite a distance for a less experienced hunter, but not for this one. He was the best, and demanded top wages for his expertise. His job? He was supposed to kill the Whip of the stagecoach. He didn't know who the Whip was, and frankly he didn't care. Five hundred dollars was five hundred dollars and he needed the cash. Regardless of his prey, he would do his job. Let the others do the follow-up.

'Got him in your sights?' the fidgeting observer lying next to the hunter asked for the second time in as many seconds.

'I'll do my part,' the hunter responded. 'I need to concentrate.'

'This is gonna work!' the observer said, his constant interruptions and the excitement in his voice irritating the hunter to the point of exasperation.

'I got him in my sights, now shut up!'

'The Boss says this is gonna work!' the observer said, his anticipation growing the closer the stagecoach came to the predetermined spot.

'Will you just shut up!' the hunter said with a stern and overly impatient edge to his voice. 'Let me concentrate...'

The observer, whose Christian name was Oliver, was not used to being silenced by anyone, let alone a member of his own gang. He immediately went quiet, but he clenched his tobacco-stained teeth, the muscles of his jaw balling and tight. His eyes grew hard as flint and he seethed in silence. He shot a glance at the man lying next to him, picturing the satisfaction he would obtain in the next few moments. That this hunter was only hired for killing the Whip didn't matter, and in fact, made things simpler. Oliver had never before let anyone live who disrespected him, and he wasn't going to start now. His father had repeatedly taught him respect and had emphasized each lesson with a belt. The lesson Oliver had learned was now as ingrained and permanent in his psyche as the scars the belt had left behind.

Trouble struck with the powerful boom from a large caliber rifle, the sound quickly evaporating like a rare morning mist in the hot desert air. The Whip felt the passing of the heavy slug as it blasted a hole in his hat and then tore off some wood molding on the back of the stagecoach before kicking up dust in the road. Whoever was shooting had just barely missed him, and the Whip knew he was in serious trouble. He leaned over, creating a smaller profile, and began yelling and snapping the reins on the rumps of his four-horse team in a desperate attempt to increase their pace.

11

A second boom sounded shortly after the first, but this one was followed by a more fleshy impact. Now closer, the angle to the target was steeper and the impact of the 405-grain bullet literally slapped the Whip heavily into the seat before he slid lifeless over the side of the stagecoach. After passing through the Whip's body the heavy and somewhat misshapen slug continued its relentless journey on through the stagecoach.

The sound of the first shot alerted Rory to potential danger. At the sound of the second shot and the sudden lurch of the stagecoach, Rory believed it was true. The danger was confirmed when Rory saw the result of the second bullet as the shadow of the Whip's body fell past the right side window. He saw where the bullet had torn through the roof of the stagecoach before splintering wood at the rear wall of the passenger compartment between the heads of the woman and the heavyset man. The faces of the two, upon seeing the ragged hole just inches from their heads, would have been comedic had it not brought the realization that death had missed them by inches. The woman reacted better than the heavy set man, who looked as if he was going to be sick. The bullet had continued on its stubborn course before lodging itself in the passengers' luggage in the boot.

Almost immediately the stagecoach lurched to the right as the front right wheel slipped off the edge of the road. The woman screamed in panic and fear as the passengers were thrown around in the enclosed space. Luckily the horses kept running forward and miraculously pulled the stagecoach back on to the road before it could roll over the side and down the slope in what would have been a spectacular crash. The horses were now running wide-eyed and spooked, not so much from the sound of the rifle but from the loss of a reassuring voice and a confident hand on the reins. Without control and direction, they were galloping frantically, pulling the stagecoach and its passengers toward an uncertain fate.

# TWO

The four travelers had boarded the Concord stagecoach back in Salt Lake City heading south at 6:00 that morning. Their path basically followed the soon-to-be-defunct Pony Express route heading south before then turning west, bound for Carson City, Nevada. The passengers hoped to join up with the approaching Central Pacific Railroad and then continue on to the coast of California by train. As soon as they started heading out the woman had become very animated, her need for conversation bubbling out of her like an artesian well.

'I guess we are going to be together for a couple of days, so I think we should get to know each other. Why don't we introduce ourselves?' she said, smiling to each of her fellow travelers in turn.

When no one volunteered any information, the woman continued, 'My name is Vivian Creed and I am from Maine. This is my first time west!' Her excitement showing on her face, and the rapidity of her speech reminded Rory of the boundless energy of a fidgeting squirrel.

Vivian shared the information that she was going to visit her uncle and patron. Her parents had died when she was very young, and her uncle had assumed her guardianship.

When she was of age, he had enrolled her in a boarding school for girls. Now in her third year at the school, her uncle had taken a position with a mining company in California and had moved west. She was going to visit him there. This was her first time west of the Mississippi and it was obvious to all present that she was very excited. Rory thought she looked older than her monologue had implied, and noting that she gave this complete monologue in less than a minute, he concluded this was going to be a very long trip indeed.

Vivian wanted to talk, so when no one else spoke up Rory thought it polite to introduce himself, if nothing more than just to appease Vivian. 'My name is Rory,' he said. 'I'm a newspaper reporter.'

When Rory would share no more, the larger of the two men then introduced himself. 'I'm Jacques Foré,' he said. 'I'm going to… to… ah… Santa Barbara, California, to set up a winery.' Obviously French by name and heavy accent, Foré was going west to seek his fortune – and his accent was not the only heavy thing about him. He was sporting a suit that had seen better days and was obviously purchased when he had far less mass, as it was now stretched tight and he was brimming over it.

Foré was sweating from just the exertion of climbing into the stagecoach, and he had a tendency to mop his bald head with a rather filthy bandanna, which he kept in his back pocket. Rory figured Mr Foré exerted himself more by his Herculean efforts to retrieve his bandanna to wipe the existing sweat than the original sweat was worth. Diminishing returns.

Mr Foré was an easy talker who enjoyed people and obviously loved food and drink. Much to everyone's dismay, including Vivian, he then began to educate his captive audience, as much as his limited English would allow, about the history of the grape. It became obvious that he seemed to know everything there was to know about grapes and the temperamental intricacies of making wine. Rory believed it wise that Foré was going on to California, as he questioned whether Foré could survive life in the West.

The marvel of the grape would have continued if Vivian had not interrupted the documentary to ask the last of her companions his name and occupation. Silence followed. Vivian was new to the West and the anonymity that the West allowed. Each of the travelers had a story, but out West it is more important what a man does than what he says. The West is vast and communication with the rest of the world was slow at best, so in the West, a man could easily lose himself accidentally... or on purpose.

Rory had known several men who had gone west to escape from their existing situation or hide from their past, but his interest always ended with the other man's silence. Anyway, Rory already knew all he needed to know about this last traveler. Vivian's innocence, however, would not be deterred, and her uncomfortable persistence finally paid off.

The holdout, who was rather unkempt and was definitely the most fragrant of the three men, finally and hesitantly spoke: 'Name's Lowe,' he said.

Rory knew Lowe – in fact Lowe was the reason Rory was even on the stagecoach. He knew Lowe was a Confederate sympathizer and was heading west carrying an important document that Rory was planning to acquire. Rory hadn't relieved him of the document as yet, for he wanted to know who Lowe's ultimate contact was.

Vivian smiled and nodded, expecting Lowe to continue his verbal offering. When nothing else was forthcoming, Vivian asked, 'Is that your first or last name?'

Lowe shot glances at the other two male passengers, either for support of western confidentiality or as a challenge to their intruding into his privacy. Rory met Lowe's eyes and just shrugged apologetically, implying Lowe was on his own. Vivian was not to be deterred and repeated her last question as if Lowe hadn't heard her. After a lengthy pause, with Vivian staring at him, he finally said, 'Last.'

Rory chuckled to himself. He felt Lowe should just give Vivian the information she craved, whether truthful or not, and end this awkward interrogation.

'Oh, so it is Mr Lowe,' Vivian said in a flirtatious manner young women often use to get their way. Feeling his answer was still incomplete, she persisted, 'You are being so formal here, Mr Lowe. We will be in this cramped stagecoach for another fifty miles so perhaps it would best if we dispensed with the formality of last names?' By turning her last statement into a question, Vivian swung the conversation again toward Lowe and reached across the narrow separation between the two facing benches and patted his knee.

That clinched it, Rory thought to himself. No way out for Lowe now.

'Oh... uh... Jack,' Lowe said, 'Jack Lowe.' Lowe then smiled at Vivian and nodded his head.

Like many out west, it was obvious to Rory that Lowe was finished sharing. Vivian didn't read this subtle termination and continued to press him for more information. But after his brief introduction Lowe just smiled, and tipping his hat over his eyes, sank back into the lurching red leather seat of the stagecoach to either sleep or feign it.

This stagecoach was a newer Concord, manufactured by Abbot and Downing. It got the name Concord as the manufacturing plant was located in Concord, New Hampshire. What made this type of stagecoach different from a standard wagon with metal spring suspension was that these coaches were slung with heavy leather straps called a thoroughbrace, and instead of bouncing up and down, they would swing slightly. Mark Twain had once described the Concord stagecoach's ride like a 'cradle on wheels'.

The ride itself was relatively comfortable, but the close proximity and smell of the passengers, the constrictive size of the carriage, and the heat and dust of the road limited any actual comfort the passengers might have enjoyed. Perhaps a slight breeze might occasionally bring relief, but the air was heating up quickly and the speed of the stage-coach was only sufficient to suspend the dust the horses' hooves kicked up.

What Rory saw, but which neither of the other two passengers seemed to have noticed, was that when Lowe had originally entered the stagecoach he was unarmed, but after their first stop to change horses in American Fork, he was now sporting two holstered six-shooters. The matching pistols, which appeared to Rory to be Army Colt .44s, were relatively common in the West. Less common was the fact that Lowe's holsters were tied down. But what really caught Rory's attention was that since the pistol barrels extended beneath their holsters he could see that the forward sights of Lowe's pistols had been removed, ensuring there would be no drag during a draw. Further, it also appeared the triggers had been removed. If the triggers were removed, Rory knew the mechanism was locked. A revolver missing both its forward sight and its trigger was designed for only one purpose: the fast draw.

This just confirmed to Rory what he had been told and had read in Lowe's dossier, which was that Lowe was a very dangerous man and a serious gunfighter. With the trigger removed and the trigger mechanism locked, Lowe need only draw back the hammer and release it to fire, in effect turning his single action revolver into less than a double action. Rory had only seen this once before with a known gunfighter he had had the misfortune to meet in Virginia – but that was some time ago, and the man was now just a statistic in some small western town's cemetery. Lowe was well heeled as a gunfighter, and Rory would need to watch him very carefully, especially when Rory made the move.

Jack Thaddeus Lowe, as Rory had previously been informed by his Captain, was a gunfighter originally from Missouri. Rory had it on good authority that Lowe was branching out and had added security services to his job qualifications, which included gunman for hire. The document Lowe carried was supposed to be the map of a lost gold mine located in the Nevada Territory, which would be used to help fund the Confederate cause.

The West was rife with the romantic legends of lost gold mines, from the Lost Dutchman Mines, supposedly located in the Superstition Mountains, to the bogus Lost Pegleg Mine, with which Rory had personal knowledge. In fact, Rory wondered whether Lowe was the recipient of one of Thomas 'Pegleg' Smith's fabricated maps.

The gold-mine myths of the west were usually based upon Spanish folklore, and the fact the Confederacy was serious exploring a mythical gold mine implied financial desperation. The Civil War was in its third year and Rory knew the Confederacy was struggling financially, but to him, counting on a long lost gold mine to help fund a war was foolishness. Still, he had his orders.

The stagecoach's cabin seemed to be designed for those less than Rory's lanky 6ft 2in frame, and he was very conscious of his large boots in the limited floor space. As Rory was sitting across from Vivian, he seemed to be the default focus of her attention. A very private individual, his introduction, like Mr Lowe's, was brief and succinct, but unlike Lowe's, Rory's was a total fabrication. Even though his story was untrue, he still obeyed the unwritten law of the West, that a man's business was his own. When Rory failed to embellish his story, Vivian took it upon herself to fill the silence for the next twenty miles.

Rory listened patiently as Vivian talked about anything and everything. Just like the stagecoach, she rattled on and on and on and on... She reminded him of the new mechanized music machines he had seen at a fair in Washington DC. It cost a penny to start the music, and once initiated, nothing could stop it until it had played itself out. Rory would have liked to have taken a nap, but he decided to be polite and feigned interest. Having ridden a stagecoach more times than he cared to remember, he knew that Vivian, like the music machines, would eventually play herself out.

Rory listened to Vivian drone on and his mind became numb to the sound of her voice. Her latest topic was about a new soap being pressed into bars and sold door to door... At least, Rory thought, Vivian was a pleasure to look at. She must have been around five foot one or two, and couldn't have weighed more than one hundred pounds dripping wet. Her hair was a blue black and her skin was extremely fair, the contrast extenuated by the brilliance of her blue eyes. She was dressed in what Rory knew was the latest fashion, with matching handkerchief and handbag, so obviously her uncle had money. But the latest fashion or not, Vivian's multilayered outfit had to be hot, and Rory could see the beginning evidence of perspiration on her brow and full upper lip.

As Rory had anticipated, Vivian played herself out around the twenty-mile mark and was now sitting numb with her eyes closed and her head tilted back. He imagined her reaction if she slipped off to sleep and started snoring. She would be horrified. He secretly hoped for that comedic scene, but he could see she wasn't falling asleep as she continued to hold the handkerchief to her nose. He figured her stock of toilet water must be nearing empty and concluded that when they had another twenty miles under their belts the lone handkerchief would be her only defense. No doubt when her toilet water ran out, she would then switch to her canteen to moisten her handkerchief.

After a particularly serious jolt Rory tilted his hat up so he could watch Vivian. As he watched her he wondered whether she would like the West. Her destination, she had shared, was Sacramento but to get there she needed to cross the Nevada desert. The desert ahead of them was more than just west, it was a rugged west. So rugged that there were only a few routes safe enough to transverse the treacherous roads, and then only during certain times of the year. It was dry three hundred and sixty-five days a year, with limited springs, which were the only places where people could settle. People talk of the money to be made in mining out west, but in fact the *real* gold out west was in water, and the knowledge of where it could be found.

# THREE

It was only a matter of time before the railroad would eliminate this stagecoach route, just as the telegraph had all but eliminated the Pony Express. Rory's intelligence report had suggested that the Central Pacific Railroad and the Union Pacific Railroad were actively heading toward each other, and the transcontinental railroad would be completed within the decade – but for now he had his orders and he would see them through, even if it meant a dusty, smelly and crowded stagecoach.

The monotony of the travel drew Rory to thoughts of home. It had been a while since he had been home to the family farm in the relatively new state of Iowa. He and his father had had the inevitable father–son face-off when he was twenty-one. After bidding goodbye to his mother with a promise to keep in touch, Rory had left for Washington DC to meet up with a friend and join the Union Army. In Washington, however, his friend had encouraged Rory to meet with an influential gentleman by the name of Allen Pinkerton, and that meeting had changed Rory's life. In fact, it had ultimately led to this unfortunate stagecoach ride.

It was the Civil War that had caused the rift between Rory and his father and had prompted him to leave his home. Rory had a natural skill with firearms, and he and his friends wanted to go and fight for the Union. Rory believed it was his duty to defend the Union. His father, however, believed that Rory's first duty was to the family, and ensuring that the farm was successful. Tension between father and son built until the Union loss at the Battle of Bull Run. Rory used the loss to justify his joining, while his father, knowing the inexperience of the troops on both sides and the ineptitude of the Union leadership, forbade him to join. That was it. His father put his foot down, and Rory, ignoring his mother's tears, decided it was time for him to strike out on his own.

Allen Pinkerton was a Scottish immigrant who created the Pinkerton National Detective Agency, and was hired to head the new Union Intelligence Service during the war. He was impressed with Rory and hired him on the spot. Pinkerton demanded a high level of performance, and not only recognized Rory's current skill level, but knew that with a little seasoning, Rory could become one of his best agents. Pinkerton also intended to encourage Rory to join the Pinkerton National Detective Agency organization once the war was over.

Rory was in his sixth month with the agency when word came through covert channels of the Confederate's gold mine project – and Rory was assigned to follow the money. Well, the money was going west, and so would he. Rory knew what awaited him, and having gone west once before, was looking forward to returning.

Hot, dry and dusty was how one of Rory's lady friends back in Washington had described the West when he told her that was where he was heading. How little she knew. She had no idea of the diversity of western lands. Majestic mountains, red rock formations, deep ravines and gorges, diverse foliage, vast plains of grass and skies that never end. Hot days and cold still nights. Brisk night skies so clear and dark that the stars were overwhelming. And when the full moon cast lunar shadows, the view was surreal.

Rory loved the West. Prior to the beginning of the Civil War, Rory had even considered making a life for himself in the West with all its varied opportunities – but that would have to wait. And now here he was, out west in a stagecoach with his target, a Confederate spy and gunman, two civilians and a driverless team of madly galloping horses.

Once the stagecoach had miraculously righted itself and the passengers had a chance to gather themselves, Rory knew what needed to be done. He looked at Foré then shook his head, thinking Vivian would actually be of more help than Foré might be. Rory then looked to Lowe. Lowe returned his look, both knowing it was up to them to control the situation. 'We either have to get a hold of the reins or we have to shoot one of the horses. Regardless, one of us has to climb out, and we have to do it now,' Rory shouted above the chaotic din.

Lowe nodded and shouted back, 'What about the shooter? That was a buffalo gun that took out the Whip. Whoever goes out there won't have a chance.'

Rory nodded. This stagecoach company was not aware of their transporting anything valuable, nor were they traveling through any particularly dangerous territory, so no shotgun messenger had been assigned to accompany them. This left the lives of the passengers in the hands of just the Whip, and with his murder, the passengers were left in a very precarious position. Rory didn't want to climb out of this rampaging stagecoach, and especially didn't want to rely upon Lowe to cover his back from the sniper. As Lowe was not offering to climb out and time was essential, as accented by the sudden bump and lurch of the stagecoach, Rory finally said, 'I'll go,' and then added, 'You'll watch my back?'

'I'll do what I can,' said Lowe, 'but I can only watch the sides.'

'Well, that's better than nothing,' Rory replied.

All the passengers knew what Rory was attempting. Rory looked at Vivian, who was ashen white as she held on to the side window frame of the stagecoach for stability. Foré was sweating. Rory put on his gloves and ensured his guns were securely looped in their holsters. When he felt he was ready, he looked at Lowe, nodded and opened the stage-coach door.

The horses were galloping frantically as Rory opened the door. The motion of the stagecoach and the passing wind made the door suddenly flip out of his grasp and flap back, smashing into the side of the stagecoach before rebounding back and forth a couple of times. The ground was passing the doorway with surprising speed, mirroring the anxiety of the horses and his own racing heart. If Rory lost his footing he knew he might not survive, as he might be run over or bounced on to the rough road before rolling down the steep embankment and onto the rocks below. He had to be very, very careful.

With a nod of his head to Lowe, Rory stood and slowly worked his way out of the door so he was standing on the door jam on his tiptoes with his back to the open door and his hands holding tightly to the sides of the door. To make matters even more challenging, the door began to bump back and forth against him with the motion of the stagecoach. He knew there was a luggage rack of sorts on the roof of the stagecoach, and this should provide decent handholds for him to climb on top – but first he had to get a hold of it.

Rory's left foot slipped out of the doorway when the stagecoach hit a rock and lurched suddenly. Vivian gasped, but Rory had been holding on to the sides of the door tightly enough that he was able to right himself almost immediately, though the danger of his situation was re-emphasized to his tense audience.

Once he had both feet firmly planted again, he jumped up and was able to get his chest on the roof of the stagecoach and grab desperately for the side of the luggage rack – but he missed. He had let go his handholds on the side of the door to make the jump, and now found himself bouncing and sliding on the roof scrambling for new handholds. Luckily there were some packages that were lashed down to the metal rack and he was able to grasp the rope and keep himself from sliding off. He slowly pulled himself up, praying the rope would hold. It held, and once he felt securely on top, he was able, for the first time, to take a breathless assessment of the situation. He saw the blood splatter and the torn up seat and molding. Yes, Lowe was correct: the large caliber bullet had made a mess.

Looking at the small hills and rock formations around him, Rory realized he was totally exposed and unprotected. He knew Lowe would be of no assistance, and that there was nothing he would be able to do, even if he did spot the sniper. He could only hope he was either out of range or wasn't worth a bullet. He was committed.

Carefully Rory crawled forward and was able finally to sit down on the blood-soaked driver's seat. The reins had fallen down and were dragging on the ground behind the horses. The horses were too frantic to be consoled by a calming voice, though Rory still kept up a calming one-sided discussion with the team, if anything just to take his mind off his precarious situation.

Like most stagecoaches and wagons, this one had a hand brake, but these brakes were more of a parking brake than the means to slowly stop a runaway. Putting the brake on and forcing its use would only weaken the brakes and possibly damage them. Anyway, Rory knew the brakes were useless at this speed.

Looking at the rigging and then at the end of the reins trailing in the dirt Rory realized there was no way he could reach the reins at either point. Climbing down on to the stagecoach's extended tongue seemed ridiculous as it was moving and bouncing unpredictably as a result of the team's panic. He had heard of individuals who had attempted this, and in every instance the daring hero had fallen off and was seriously injured or killed. To consider leaping on to the back of one of the rear horses was also ridiculous. As it seemed the only viable option, he was seriously considering shooting one of the horses. He was repulsed with the idea of shooting, wounding, and eventually killing a horse just to use it as a brake, but the lives of those on the stagecoach were more important. He also knew he would have to shoot the horse in such a way that it died slowly, and forced the others to also slow down, basically hobbling the team. He also concluded that he might have to shoot both the rear horses to make the drag uniform. Shooting just one horse was dangerous, because if it stumbled or collapsed it might disrupt the forward direction of the stagecoach, causing it to veer off the road and crash.

Rory positioned himself to shoot the left rear horse in the hindquarters when out of the corner of his eye he saw the driver's whip. Stagecoach drivers were called Whips, especially in California, and they got their name from the long whip they carried as part of their equipment. These whips were not used to drive so much as to impress the passengers with their lively and loud crack. Rory personally knew one Whip who was constantly practicing cracking his whip for that very purpose. Whips would get paid by their employers, but they would also receive presents from those they drove, especially if the passenger was someone important or famous. Gifts of choice included fancy white fringed gloves, the most popular gift, followed by finely tooled boots, spurs, large ornamented hats and of course ornamented whips such as the one owned by the now dead Whip of this stagecoach. These gifts elevated a Whip's status amongst his fellows and were highly desirable.

This Whip's whip, a thought that Rory found amusing, especially in light of the situation, was longer and sturdier than the standard stock whip, and reminded Rory of the two-handed bullock whip popular in Australia, though not quite as long. It was highly ornamented and sported multi-colored braided leather. Rory knew that most stock whips had a large butt knot with a wrist loop on the end of the stock or handle, which was used for hanging it up, as no Whip worth his salt would ever lay his precious whip on the ground or lean it in a corner. Whips were status and were meant to be displayed, and this one had no doubt been a treasured possession.

Rory thought he might be able to retrieve the reins if this whip had the typically large butt knot on the end. He grabbed the whip out of its tube, and found that Lady Luck was smiling upon him as the butt knob was substantial.

Wrapping the popper and as much of the leather thong of the whip as possible around his right hand and then taking hold of the whip's keeper, he carefully lay down on the driver's box footrest and leaned as far forward as he felt was safe – it would be in no one's interest, especially his, if he bounced forward and fell under the stagecoach. The stagecoach was bouncing and weaving back and forth with the panic-stricken gallop of the horses, and Rory wasn't sure this was the best method to get control of the team, but he felt he had to give it a try. He could always shoot a horse as a last resort. Time and time again he tried, but just as he managed to lift the reins the stagecoach would give a jump and the reins would slide off the whip.

The stagecoach suddenly hit a spot where the road was slightly washed out, a place the Whip would have easily avoided, but the frantic horses raced right over it. The following jar almost tossed Rory from the driver's box and under the out-of-control stagecoach. Only a truly desperate grab saved him, and it was a double miracle that he still managed to hold on to the whip.

Once the stagecoach had settled, Rory heard Lowe call from inside: 'Rory, you still there?'

'Barely,' Rory responded, shaking in an adrenalin rush, realizing he had almost gone under the wagon: if he had,

Lowe and the other passengers would surely have felt the additional lurch as the stagecoach crushed him beneath the wheels. He wondered whether Lowe's asking was really to inquire after his welfare, or to determine another method of approach.

As time passed and his frustration mounted, Rory was about to give up, when everything suddenly fell into place – the distance and position of the reins, the bounce of the stagecoach and the motion of the whip's butt knot. Lady Luck had finally blessed his efforts as the butt knot caught the reins! Now he just had to bring them up without losing them. Agonizingly slowly he pulled the whip back, his heart jumping with every lurch of the stagecoach. When he almost had the reins in his hand, the stagecoach suddenly lurched, causing the whip to bounce – and Rory could only watch helplessly as the reins once again slipped off the butt knot and fell back on to the road. He had to start all over again. Blessing his efforts? No, Lady Luck was mocking him.

By now the horses had been running madly for a while and were no longer running as a team, but were fighting against each other in desperation. Their disjointed galloping caused the stage to lurch even more, which further hindered Rory's attempts to snag the reins. His biggest fear now was that one of the horses would falter, causing the others to trip and forcing the stage to tongue down and roll. He decided he would try just one more time to snag the reins, and if it didn't work, he would start shooting horses.

What he then thought took forever was actually only a few seconds at best, when he again managed to snag the reins – but this time he was successful in bringing them to hand! Once seated in the driver's box and with the reins secured in his hand, he began to slow the team. The pressure and control of the reins coupled with his calming yet stern voice finally brought the team to a lathered and trembling halt.

# FOUR

The hunter had done his job, the Whip was dead. He was pleased with himself whenever he made such a good shot and at such a considerable distance. He knew he was the best, which was why he could demand $500. He just needed to get his money and leave. He didn't like the job or the company, and the sooner he left, the sooner he felt he could purge the image of the Whip from his soul, not to mention the knowledge that there were passengers within the stagecoach. He had convinced himself over and over again that what he would see through his peep sight was simply a target, just like the buffalo he slaughtered by the thousands.

But he was wrong, and the faces wouldn't leave his mind. He now hoped a very hot bath, a bottle and the right company would help him forget. He had accepted this job as he needed the cash, and now he just wanted to leave this place and its vivid memory. He would have been gone by now, but his irritating observer was too busy watching the fate of the driverless stagecoach careering along to give him his money. He had been assured he would get his money as soon as he had made the kill.

Oliver had watched with satisfaction when the driver's body took the bullet and flopped over the side. His heart soared as the stagecoach lurched suddenly when its front left wheel left the road. He fully expected it to slip over the side of the road in a spectacular crash. From there it would only be a matter of getting what his Boss was after amongst the death and debris. But to his dismay, the stagecoach amazingly righted itself and continued its erratic path down the road at a fast gallop.

'Son of a gun,' Oliver said as he sat up, disappointment dripping like the sweat his excitement had previously elicited. 'It didn't crash!'

'Ain't my problem,' the hunter expressed. 'I did my job. The Whip is dead. Now I want my money.' The hunter sat up expectantly as he inspected his rifle, removing and saving the brass cartridges and blowing out the action.

'Good for you, but the stagecoach didn't crash,' Oliver lamented as he watch the stagecoach pass by their snipping position and head further down the road. His anger grew even worse when he saw one of the passengers climb on top of the stagecoach and after some acrobatic heroics somehow took control of the frantic horses. 'This really messes things up!' he said. 'Hey, why don't you shoot some of the horses?'

'Again, ain't my problem. Just give me what's owed and I'm gone.'

'Give me your rifle and I'll shoot 'em! Hurry, before they're out of range!' Oliver demanded.

'No one uses this rifle but me,' the hunter said with an edge to his voice.

'The Boss ain't going to be pleased.'

34

'Not my problem. I did what I was contracted for, and now I just want my money.'

'You are getting on my nerves,' Oliver said as he got up from his sitting position and prepared to mount his horse. 'Now we'll have to do it the hard way.'

'You ain't leaving,' the hunter declared, his irritation growing, 'not till I get my money.'

'You want to get paid?' Oliver said with his back to the hunter.

'Yea, I do.'

'Okay.' And with that, Oliver turned with his gun drawn and put two bullets into the hunter's chest.

The force of the bullets drove the hunter back on to the ground. He attempted to pull his own side arm but Oliver shot him again. 'You basta…' the hunter started to say, but was unable to finish before his eyes glazed over and he slowly lay back on to the dirt, the air leaving his lungs in a slow, anguished and bubbly hiss. His last haunting thought was the look on the desperate Whip's face through the peep sight as he pulled the trigger – and then there was nothing.

'Well, at least this part of the plan worked,' Oliver said to the lifeless body before him. 'I gotta tell the Boss about the stagecoach, but afore I do, I'm gonna see what you got on you 'sides that sweet rifle. After that, it's just you and them buzzards.'

\*\*\*\*

It took Rory nearly a mile to get the stagecoach stopped. Once he had succeeded, he quickly hopped down and went to calm and reassure the lathered and quivering horses. The other passengers shakily climbed out of the stagecoach, their faces exhibiting relief and gratitude. Both Vivian and Lowe came over and thanked Rory for his actions on their behalf, while Foré was sitting on the stage-coach step, sweating profusely and endeavoring to keep himself from vomiting.

Once Vivian had left to calm and reassure Foré, Lowe quickly said to Rory: 'I heard three shots whilst you was out there. Two almost at the same time, followed by another shot. They weren't no buffalo gun neither, and they weren't aimed at the stagecoach. Smaller caliber, I think maybe a 44. What do you think is going on Rory?'

'I have no idea. The Whip was shot by someone lying in wait. Whoever it was shot twice from the front, and based upon the bullet's trajectory, he was slightly elevated. The fact that he shot twice so quickly and so accurately means he was very, very good and he knew what he are doing.'

Lowe looked closely at Rory and asked, '...bullet *trajectory*?'

Rory shrugged and said, 'You can determine the location of the shooter by observing the path of the bullet. I recently wrote an article about this new science of what they are beginning to call forensics.'

'Who are "they"?' Lowe asked.

'You know, police investigators.'

'I guess that makes sense. So using this *trajectory*, where was the shooter?' Lowe asked making sure he pronounced the word correctly, and with flavored skepticism seeping into his voice.

Rory ignored the skepticism and continued, 'Well, the first bullet hit the molding on the back of the stagecoach as it was torn up, so that means the shooter was higher than the stagecoach and he was shooting down, correct?'

Lowe nodded in agreement, and Rory continued, 'That first shot must have alerted the Whip, which explains why he yelled suddenly and started galloping the team. I imagine the second bullet must have hit the driver, probably in the chest as it left a bloody hole in the seat cushion and then continued into the coach, passing between Vivian and Foré, barely missing both. Knowing the position of the Whip, the bullet had to have again come from forward and high, but even higher than the previous shot. So the angle became sharper, which implies we were getting closer to the shooter's position and he had to increase his downward angle. I imagine the shots probably came from that small hill topped with rocks we drove around a few miles back. It was the perfect spot to shoot the Whip, for the road headed straight toward that hill for a while before skirting around it. A shooter on that hill would have had several seconds of straight shooting opportunity.'

Lowe considered this for a moment, then finally nodded in acceptance. Then he asked, 'What I don't understand is, why shoot the Whip? I mean it makes no sense. Why shoot the Whip unless the shooter wanted us to crash?'

'You know, that wouldn't be such a bad idea if you were planning on robbing the stagecoach,' Rory stated unemotionally. 'Shooting the Whip and causing the stagecoach to crash would kill or severely injure the passengers. Then the robbers would just come in and take what they wanted. No armed confrontation from armed passengers.'

Lowe was watching Rory closely as Rory was analyzing the situation. Rory continued, 'I know I am not about to let anyone rob me, and...' Rory paused, and looking into Lowe's eyes said, 'And seeing your outfit, I doubt you would either, so causing a crash would be the easiest way.'

'Makes sense, I reckon,' Lowe commented, still eyeing Rory.

'Efficient, but cold-hearted,' Rory said – then seeing Lowe staring at him, continued, 'I'll need to take notes about this, as my readers won't believe this really happened to me. This is just like an episode out of one of those dime novels.'

Lowe considered this, and then chuckling, said: 'Be sure you write about you climbing out and bringing the stagecoach to a stop. You saved us all,' he said with a grudging admiration. After a second he continued, 'You know, I've been pondering on that shot. There ain't a lot that could have made that shot. I figger a hundred fifty, maybe two hundred yards?'

'If we were supposed to crash, I was wondering what they were hoping to collect,' Rory added. 'I mean, why go to this trouble? We're not carrying a payroll, bank bag or gold transfer, at least that I know. The stagecoach company didn't even bother sending an armed messenger riding shotgun to accompany us, and unless one of us is hiding something, which the robbers somehow know about, they'd find very little to make it worth the effort. I know I'm not carrying anything that valuable, and I doubt Miss Vivian or Foré are. Are you?'

Rory watched Lowe carefully for any tell. He knew Lowe would not be forthcoming, but he wanted to see if he got nervous with his summation. Lowe was good. He was quiet, as if considering something, then silently shook his head. He then shared a thought that was also in the back of Rory's mind. 'If'n that was to be a robbery attempt, you know they'll hit us again.'

'I know, and I'm worried,' Rory said. 'We can't expect help this far from the way station, and when we don't make our scheduled stop, it'll be a day, maybe two, before the company sends someone to investigate.'

'You think you can drive the stagecoach to the next station?' asked Lowe.

'The horses look all in, but I'll check them over,' Rory said. 'If they can't make it to the next way station, we'll need to find a place to lay low for the night. Let's drive the stagecoach a little further and look for a place to hole up, one that is defensible.'

'Sounds good. You drive, I'll ride shotgun,' Lowe said, turning away while stating he was going to get his rifle from his luggage. But he came back shortly, his face red with anger. 'That shot that killed the Whip, the one that went through the cabin, it got stopped by the stock of my rifle!' he said with muted anger, holding up the splintered stock of his now useless rifle. 'It's ruined!'

'That's too bad. The loss of your rifle means less long range protection. Does Foré have a weapon?' Rory asked doubtfully.

Lowe shook his head, 'He's a tenderfoot. Good he's going on to California. Just look at him over there, sweating like a pig and trying to hold on to his breakfast.'

Rory felt sorry for Foré, but he also knew Foré was unaccustomed to this type of danger. 'Loosen your loop, Lowe. Foré may be a tenderfoot, but he might prove himself in time.' 'If he lives long enough,' Lowe said with dry humor.

Rory took Lowe's rifle and looked over the mechanism. 'A Henry,' Rory said admiringly. 'It takes that new brass .44 cartridge?'

'This really chaps my hide!' said Lowe angrily. 'I just got this rifle. I love the ease of using the metal cartridges. I was talking to a gunsmith friend of mine and he was saying he believed he could convert my new Colt Army .44 to use the same ammunition. It would sure be a faster reload and save a pack of money.'

'I know what you mean,' Rory said as he inspected Lowe's Henry. 'You just need a new stock,' he said with confidence, 'then it'll be good as new.'

'Yea, but I need the iron now, not when I get to replacing the stock.'

To ease Lowe's anger and to make conversation Rory commented, 'Just like you wanted, I had my weapons converted to use the same .44 cartridge.'

Lowe then turned back to Rory, 'You got a rifle?' Rory nodded and went to get his rifle from his luggage. Lowe looked at Rory in surprise when he handed him his rifle. It was also a Henry, but with a few special modifications.

'Nice weapon,' Lowe said as he worked the action and admired its smoothness. 'This is a rather uncommon long gun. It looks like it has been enhanced by a knowing hand. Your work?' he asked.

Rory looked at Lowe, realizing he had just handed Lowe his custom weapon, which had just been issued to him by the agency. He should have been more careful because Lowe wasn't stupid, and the last thing Rory needed was for Lowe to start questioning who he was, based on the uniqueness and quality of his weapons.

Lowe kept looking the rifle over, and Rory knew he had to divert Lowe's attention lest he become suspicious. 'It was a gift from my editor,' Rory said. 'He gave it to me when I left for this assignment. He is the one who arranged to have my Colts converted to the .44.' Then retrieving his rifle from Lowe, and trying to switch his attention further away from his rifle he said, 'Let's tell the others what we are planning, and see if either of them are carrying.'

'You can ask, but I doubt either of them is heeled,' Lowe stated. 'And I think you are right, we should head out as soon as possible. We need to get as far away from this area as we can.'

While Lowe went to put the ruined remains of his rifle back in the boot, Rory went to check the team. The horses were still nervous, but he gave each of the team a quick inspection and a pat on the neck. He then got a water bucket from the boot, and filling it from the small water barrel stored in the back, began to water the horses. The team looked good, and the water did wonders for their spirits. He then checked the rigging and moved on to the stagecoach itself. Everything looked in working condition in spite of their frantic ride. He was just going to suggest that perhaps they could drive the team on to the next station after all, when he noticed one of the front wheels didn't look plumb. It was the front wheel that had slipped over edge of the road during the horses' mad gallop. Getting down on his knees he looked underneath, and to his dismay, he could see a visible crack in the forward axel. The crack was at least half way through the axel, and just the weight of the stagecoach was spreading it. He had seen this type of crack temporarily reinforced with raw hide, but unfortunately there was none available.

The damaged axel changed everything. To avoid further cracking and possible breakage, the stagecoach would have to be driven very slowly and stay only on the smoothest parts of the road. He knew that any jar could split that axel completely, and the group would be stranded and at the mercy of those attempting to rob them when they came back to finish the job.

When Lowe returned, Rory show him the axel. Lowe swore, then added, 'You think that axel will last until we get to a safer location?'

'What choice do we have?' Rory asked.

'We could each ride a horse the rest of the way to the next way station,' Lowe suggested.

'You think Vivian or better yet, Mr Foré could ride bareback for twenty-five miles on a skittish horse?' Rory asked, a growing smirk on his face. 'I doubt these horses are that saddle broke.'

Lowe almost laughed out loud when he thought of the idea. 'Yea, I see your point!' Then after a second of humorous reflection he said, 'It's too bad there are no trees around here, as we might build a travois and drag him. Of course they would have to be pretty big trees!'

'Yea,' Rory said with a chuckle, feeling a little guilty for sharing a laugh at Foré's expense. 'Okay then, we'll find a place to hole up for the night?'

'I think that's best,' Lowe said. 'Let's inform the others and go as far as we can,'

'I think it would be better if we lessened any additional load on that axle. I think you should all walk, and we need to unload any unnecessary weight,' Rory suggested.

Soon Vivian, Foré and Lowe were standing next to the lightened stagecoach, with the luggage now stacked on the side of the road. Once Rory was seated in the box, he slapped the reins on the horses' backs and they slowly moved out. Rory had to rein back on the horses, for they wanted to proceed at their normal gait, but he held them back for fear of breaking the crippled axel.

It was late afternoon and they had traveled about two miles when Lowe pointed to a jumble of very large rocks just off the road about another mile distant. The spot was next to one of the many short cliffs of sandstone, typical of the Great Basin desert. At the designated spot, Rory slowly drove the stagecoach off the road and within the odd circle of boulders. Like the cliffs, the boulders were also of sandstone, having fallen from the short cliff above, cut, over time, by the elements. Many were of a significant size, such that a man could easily take refuge behind them. These boulders looked like they might provide a defensible place to park the wagon. With each shifting of the front axel as they rode amongst the boulders Rory expected to hear a splintering crack as the fractured axel finally gave out. Their luck held as they arrived safely, axel intact.

Once he had stopped the stagecoach, Rory stood up and surveyed the surroundings. The boulders did indeed form a parameter of sorts, from which all approaches could be watched, and except for some creosote bush there was no useful ground cover for approaching enemies. Rory had driven the stagecoach carefully within the ring of rock and parked it broadside, parallel to the road and back in against the cliff. He unhitched the horses and ground staked them behind the stagecoach to provide them as much protection as possible. He even found a little grass there, and the horses quickly went to work.

Not one to be idle, Vivian organized their meager supplies and then went over to Foré who was sitting on a rock, flushed and sweating. Lowe walked over to Rory and said, pointing at Foré: 'He is worthless.'

'Maybe,' Rory said. Then changing the subject said, 'You got yourself a good eye for defense.'

Lowe looked around and grunted, 'It's okay.'

'I think we can defend this place until the stagecoach company comes looking for us,' Rory said. 'We got water and ammunition, and if we pool our food, we could last several days, which will be more than enough.'

'I told Foré and Vivian to gather brushwood for a fire, should we need one,' Lowe said. 'Vivian gave me a "who put you in charge" look, and Foré was just sweating. Not the best team, but they will work.'

'Perhaps asking for their help would be better than just giving orders,' Rory said. 'Anyway, gathering what little wood there might be is a good idea. At dusk, I think we should avoid any movement and position ourselves to cover the perimeters.'

'Okay, you're right about giving the others orders,' Lowe admitted grudgingly; then asked Rory: 'So when should we build the fire?'

'It'll get chilly tonight, but not cold. I think we should set up a fire but not light it unless we are attacked,' Rory shared.

'Why light the fire only if attacked?' Lowe asked.

'Out here our camp will be harder to find without a fire, and if we only light the fire when we are attacked, it will basically blind our attackers and make it harder for them to differentiate our muzzle flashes,' Rory offered. 'We'll be able to see them better than they will see us with a glaring light. As long as we don't backlight ourselves the fire will give us a tactical advantage.'

'I like the way you think, Rory. I think I'll empty a few cartridges at the base of the wood pile to cause a quick flare up when it's lit,' Lowe said.

'Good idea. Just let everyone know not to look into the flames when it goes up!' Rory suggested.

'Yea. You got that right!' Lowe said with a friendly chuckle.

# FIVE

The observer arrived back at the meeting place leading the hunter's horse. He was carrying the hunter's Sharps, his holster and short guns, a silver pocket watch and fob, and about $150 cash. Thirteen additional men were gathered around a small fire when he rode up.

One of the men standing on the outskirts of the camp and watching the rider approach, exclaimed, 'Well, if it ain't Olivia.' Then turning to the fire he called out in a mocking tone, 'It's Olivia. He's finally decided to show his ugly face.'

'Shut up, Casper,' the man being mockingly addressed as Olivia said as he dismounted. After he tied the two horses to a convenient bush, and taking up his new rifle, he walked toward the others.

'Yea, well you make me,' the obstinate man responded, ridiculing the newcomer as he jogged over to continue his verbal attack. 'Oliver, that is such a prissy name. Named after a fruit!'

'Better than Cassssssssper. You named after an ass?'

'Shut your trap,' Casper replied. Then in a threatening tone he exclaimed, 'One of these days I'm gonna remove your lying tongue.'

'You're welcome to try any time you feel lucky.'

'Luck's got nothing to do with me airing out your hide.'

'They're at it again, Boss,' one of the other men, known simply as Ranger, said to the Boss, who was the only man seated at the fire.

'Shut up, the both of you,' the seated man said with a clipped southern accent. 'I can't believe you two are brothers.'

'Half-brothers, Boss. Older by nine months!' said Casper with menace in his voice and a stiffness to his jaw. Then raising his voice and throwing a challenge to his half-brother, 'Your pa was a drunkard Mex.'

'And yours was a murdering Sioux,' Oliver hissed back. 'I guess that makes you a half-breed as well as a half-brother so that makes you only a quarter man!'

'Why you…'

'That's enough. Those are the same barbs you always throw at each other,' the seated man said. 'Either come up with some new, funnier cracks or get it over with and just kill each other. Just do it after this job is done.' Then turning to Oliver he quietly asked, 'Well?'

'He shot the Whip clean as a whistle but the stagecoach didn't crash. The horses bolted and the stagecoach started to go over the edge but it somehow righted itself and kept on the road. Then one of the passengers plays hero and climbs out and fetches the reins and they ride off.'

The Boss swore under his breath. Casper, listening in, asked, 'Why didn't that old buffalo hunter just shoot a horse? That would have caused a crash,' he volunteered before walking forward and rejoining the rest of the gang.

'I suggested it,' Oliver said, 'but he said he was con-tracted for the Whip and only the Whip. Then turns into

47

some kinda horse lover – but he ain't around no more.'
Then turning to the Boss he said, 'Saved you five hundred
dollars, Boss!'

'Did you see where the coach stopped?' the Boss asked.

'No, but that team was charging full steam and I bet
they're now plain tuckered out, so I'm sure they took a rest
once they got clear of the area. I bet they'll spend the night
there as well.'

'Very good. We'll have to plan a raid for tonight under
the cover of darkness. At least we seem to have stopped
them close to the midway point between stations to give us
the most time and opportunity. It'll be a little more difficult now, but we'll still get the goods.'

The Boss then walked away from the group with Oliver
in tow. When they were out of hearing distance Oliver said,
'So Boss, what are the goods? They didn't have a messenger riding shotgun.'

'You leave that to me,' the Boss confided.

'We'd better watch out for the man that took control of
the coach,' Oliver said. 'He looked young but salty.'

Oliver turned back to get some supplies from his horse
when his Boss asked, 'So what plunder did the Hunter
donate to our cause besides his rifle?'

The question caused Oliver to pause slightly but he
came back quickly with, 'Just a brace of very used and very
old short irons, his horse and outfit, a pocket watch, and a
couple of bucks.'

'The boys can divvy up everything but bring me the cash
and give me the rifle.'

'Ah Boss, I was kinda hoping I could keep the rifle for
myself.'

'Perhaps, but for now the rifle stays with me.'

'Okay, Boss,' Oliver said, as he reluctantly handed over the Sharps.

'So how much money did he have on him?' the Boss asked.

'I'm not really sure, let me go get it.'

'Bring it all over here, Oliver,' the Boss said, with an emphasis on the word 'all'.

Oliver went to his horse and returned a short time later with the rifle, revolvers, pocket watch and $50 in cash. 'Is that all the cash he had on him?' the Boss asked incredulously.

'That's all I could find,' Oliver replied, straight-faced.

'He had to have more than $50 because I gave him $150 advance. You check for a money belt?"

Oliver swore under his breath. He should have remembered the Boss had given the hunter an advance. Now he would have to go back to the body and pretend the rest of the money was in a money belt or face the wrath of the Boss.

Oliver hesitated and then slowly shook his head. 'Sorry, Boss, I didn't think to check for a money belt.' Then without thinking it through, he asked, 'But what if he doesn't have a money belt?'

'He'd better have a money belt if all you could find was $50. If he doesn't then you'd better figure out where the rest of the money went,' the Boss said with an edge to his voice.

'Ah… Yea Boss,' Oliver said, knowing the Boss was giving him a way out of his dilemma. 'I'm sure he had a money belt, and I'll get the rest of the money in the morning.'

The Boss approached him, and Oliver cringed when the Boss put his arm around his shoulders and got so close that Oliver could feel his breath on his face as he said, 'See that you do, but not tomorrow, you need to leave before it gets dark', the underlying threat obvious to both. Then leading Oliver along, the two rejoined the others around the fire. The rest of the gang watched the Boss and Oliver enter the circle with the confident appraising eyes of experience and expectation. Each of the men was confident in their abilities and sense of tough equality – all, that is, except Oliver and Casper, who in addition had eyes that were windows of hatred and loathing aimed at each other.

'The buffalo hunter shot clean, but the stagecoach somehow righted itself and continued on,' the Boss explained to the others. 'To make matters worse, a passenger climbed out and got control of the stagecoach. Last we know they headed out.'

'I thought you said that without the Whip the stagecoach would go off the road and crash!' one of the gang said.

'That was my thinking, but...'

'It actually started to go over, but it somehow righted itself,' Oliver interjected.

'Well, why didn't you shoot the horses or are you too stupid to figure that out?' Casper said with contempt, knowing Oliver had already addressed that issue privately, but now he wanted to raise the issue in front of the gang just to discredit his half-brother.

Oliver immediately turned to Casper and threw a right into Casper's face. It was just a glancing blow, as Casper had turned slightly, dodging in reaction. Even so, it still caused Casper to step back and he almost went to his knees. It would have been better for both of them if Casper had gone down, as pride would have been satisfied, but Casper just shook his head and dove into Oliver's gut, so both went down in a tangle of arms and legs. The two struggled a bit on the ground, clamoring for position and kicking up considerable dust, until Casper somehow managed to end up on top and ripped a right into Oliver's face. In desperation Oliver arched his back, forcing Casper off and struggling to their feet – the two combatants then circled warily before they attacked each other, throwing wicked punches back and forth.

The other members of the gang eagerly began to gather around the battling men, cheering on their favorite. The Boss came over, and observing the two men, calmly stated, 'Five dollars Casper draws first blood.'

'You got it, Boss,' said a rather unkempt and heavy-bearded man named Mason.

'Whose holding the money?' said a very tall and lean man named Roscoe as he raised a bill: 'I've got ten on Casper!'

The two fighting men were oblivious of the cheering crowd as they let loose with a hatred that had been building for some time. Each considered the other a reminder of the negativity of questionable parentage, each believing that the other somehow added to their own embarrassment, each determined to restore respectability with the defeat of the other. Each was lost in a cloud of focused rage, so focused they seemed impervious to pain, willing to take punishment as long as they were able to administer it as well.

'All right, that's enough,' the Boss said as he motioned for two of the audience to finally separate the two combatants.

'Ah, come on, Boss. This has been building for some time. Why not let them blow it off?' Mason said, accompanied by a chorus of agreement.

'No. We have work to do and we need everybody to do it.'

Both men were covered in dirt and both were breathing heavily as they were finally pulled apart. Though separated they continued to struggle to get at each other. Oliver was sporting a reddening scuff on his face, and a mouse was forming under his left eye. Casper's nose was bleeding. Irritated at losing $10 to Mason, the Boss roared again for the two men to stop. The two men resented being pulled apart and were ready go at it again, but they were being held tightly. 'Looks like you owe me ten bucks, Boss,' Mason said as he held on to the struggling Casper.

Soon the gang was distributing bets won and owed.

'Lucky the Boss saved your bacon, Olivia,' Casper said, wiping the blood from his nose on to his sleeve. Oliver made one last lunge at Casper before the Boss yelled, 'Enough! We've got a job to do, so let's get it done. After that you can do what you want.'

Once everyone had finally settled down, the Boss flipped a $10 gold piece to Mason, who deftly caught the coin in his left hand before the Boss continued, 'Now that the entertainment is over, we need to make plans. It seems our original plan failed. The stagecoach didn't crash. Worse yet, one of the passengers played the hero and climbed out and got the stagecoach under control.'

'You think they made it to the next station?' asked a dark-skinned and very heavy man named Rodrigo in a prominent Mexican accent.

'Those team horses really ran themselves,' Oliver said in response to Rodrigo's question. 'I doubt they would have made it to the next station.'

'So where are they now?' Rodrigo asked. No sooner did the question leave his mouth when the group heard a solitary gunshot.

'I think that answers your question, Rodrigo,' the Boss said. 'Now get some grub going Rodrigo, and the rest of you get ready for action tonight.' Then taking Oliver aside he said, 'Go, while you still have light, and find their location, then do the other errands we talked about. You be sure and come back with answers.'

'Okay, Boss.'

\*\*\*\*

It was late afternoon and the sun was descending, yet heatwaves still molded the air in the distance. Rory and Lowe were determining defensive positions, while Vivian and Foré were gathering anything with which to build a fire. The stillness was suddenly shattered by a terrified scream, followed by shouting from Vivian. Both Rory and Lowe reacted and ran in the direction of the commotion. Typical of Rory, he drew his revolver on the run. With Rory outrunning Lowe, they both closed in on the traumatized pair who were being serenaded by a familiar warning rattle.

As Rory arrived, Vivian pointed to a large diamondback that was coiled at Foré's feet and giving him a rattling death stare. Foré was standing motionless, holding a few pieces of dried brush he had gathered and which had disturbed the now highly irritated viper. Rory saw that Foré was smart enough not make any sudden movements, though it appeared he was weaving a bit, and it looked like he might soil himself. The snake was good size and its rattle was a blur of motion.

Rory had stopped and was assessing the situation when Lowe arrived. Immediately Lowe drew and fired in one blur of motion. The snake jerked to the side, its body flipping in the air, landing twitching, headless and bleeding across Foré's feet. Before the sound of the shot had even begun to fade, Lowe had reholstered his gun and Foré had collapsed in a dead faint. Rory went to help Vivian with the unconscious Foré while Lowe went and picked up the still twitching snake. The snake was long and thick.

'A grandpa snake with fifteen rattles intact,' Lowe commented as he inspected the dripping corpse. Lifting the snake to eye level he said, 'A good five feet of tasty!'

'Nice shot, but I wish you hadn't made it,' Rory said. 'If whoever shot the Whip is still around, they now know we are as well, and they might now have our approximate location.'

'And what would you have done?' Lowe asked, his voice carrying an edge of taunting.

'We could have tried distracting the snake,' Rory replied.

'You think Foré could have waited that long?'

'Maybe, but we'll never know, will we?'

'He's a tenderfoot,' Lowe said. 'He would have fainted right on the critter and we'd be burying him instead of trying to revive him.'

'Perhaps,' Rory said before turning to avoid further debate. He had just confirmed more of what he had read about Lowe prior to his embarking on this assignment. Lowe was extremely fast and deadly accurate. He was also extremely confident in his ability, almost to the point of arrogance. Rory doubted Lowe would hesitate to kill, even if just to prove his superiority. Lowe was shaping up to be quite an adversary. In a fair duel, Rory was not sure he could take him, at least not without both of them getting shot... and possibly killed.

# SIX

It didn't take long for Oliver to locate the stagecoach, especially after hearing the gunshot, but he first went to where the Whip had been shot and tracked the stagecoach forward. Of course after finding the Whip he emptied the dead driver's pockets and collected anything else of value. He debated with himself about taking the Whip's boots and hat, but he tried on the boots and unfortunately they were too small. The hat was not his style, not to mention there was now a bullet hole in the crown. It was a nice hat though, even with the bullet hole. Apparently the Hunter's first shot didn't really miss after all, Oliver thought, it was just a couple inches too high.

Oliver noticed the exit wound on the corpse and was surprised how large and jagged it was. Obviously the heavy slug had become deformed after striking the Whip. Maybe hit a rib on its way through, he concluded. Death was quick. Lucky.

Taking what he wanted, Oliver left the corpse to disappear like many others the West absorbed. He then followed the road and finally found the stagecoach nestled in a rough semicircle of boulders backed up to a sandstone cliff just a few yards from the road. Oliver's horse was a buckskin gelding and he hoped it would blend in with the dusty brown surroundings. He dismounted and walked his mount very slowly so as not to kick up any dust. He walked, tucked next to the same cliff that ran along the road for some distance, hoping he couldn't be seen while he approached to observe the layout. He wished he had a telescope. Casper had one and Oliver was jealous of it, another reason to dislike his half-brother.

The stagecoach was in the back of the rocks and Oliver believed the horses were behind it. He was at least a hundred yards away, but he could still make out figures moving between the rocks. They had chosen well, and Oliver had to admire their caution, but there were still weaknesses, especially if they were tinhorns.

Oliver didn't know about the other passengers, but he knew one man was salty. He mentally named this man 'Lucky Hero'. The Lucky Hero was young and tall with dark hair and seemed to be in good shape. Oliver had a second to see this man's face and bearing when he performed his acrobatics in bringing the stagecoach to a halt. It took guts to climb out and on to the roof of the stagecoach when it was bouncing and moving so fast. He should have tried to shoot the man, but he didn't have a rifle, and he was sure he would have missed even though the man and the stagecoach had passed underneath his sniper's perch by not more than twenty-five yards. He could have kicked himself for not trying, but he was too involved in the drama unfolding beneath him. Using the whip to retrieve the reins was an unexpected twist.

Studying the camp Oliver saw there were three other individuals besides Lucky Hero. Oliver chuckled at that deserved nickname as he had been sure the man was going to die in his attempt to stop the runaway stagecoach – but the man was lucky and heroic. He wasn't someone Oliver would ever want to play cards against.

Now Oliver could see Lucky Hero speaking with another man. Oliver couldn't see details this far away but the other man also carried himself well. True western men carried themselves with a confident manner, or swagger. He wasn't sure why this appeared true, but in Oliver's experience it seemed that it was. Maybe it was the hard life that toughened them up, or just the confidence of capability. Either way, this second man didn't appear to be a tinhorn either. He was older than Lucky Hero and carried a brace of short guns on his hips. This might prove problematic if there were two salty men to contend with.

Oliver now noticed two other individuals who appeared to be collecting brushwood, which confirmed they would be staying the night. One of the two was a very large fat man, probably as fat as Rodrigo, and the other was, was… a woman? It was growing dark and he feared to get any closer lest he be discovered, but he was confident the second individual was a woman as her gown had a bustle. Oliver appreciated a good bustle. Well, that might change things. So there were four individuals and one of them was a woman.

Oliver watched as one man looked to be distributing guns. The darkness now prevented him from confirming this, but he believed it was Lucky Hero. So they were preparing some sort of defense? He wondered whether that would include placing a guard. Probably not. The Boss had said these passengers were tinhorns, but now he wasn't so sure. He wished he could just pick the man off, as that would save everybody a lot of trouble. He observed the man meet with the other salty man, and then the two parted and appeared to be taking up positions in the front. As he watched, it looked like the woman was instructing the fat man about the use of a rifle. Now that was odd, Oliver thought, the woman was teaching the fat man. A woman teaching firearms? Not likely. Now he knew some women were mighty fine shots, but they were rare indeed. A woman teaching firearms. The Boss was right – this had to be a tinhorn group.

The light was failing and he wanted to get back and make his report before it got dark, but he stayed and watched until the light was gone. He expected them to light a fire as they had been gathering wood. He waited at least another hour, but no fire. He then wondered whether they had food and water. They had all at some time or another visited the stagecoach so maybe that was their makeshift chuck wagon. Well, no fire and the night was well on. He couldn't see without any light so he carefully led his horse back the way he had come to ensure he made no sound. Sound carries in the cool, flat desert night.

Oliver was pleased with himself. He was returning with valuable information which might cause the Boss to alter his plans for tonight. How the Boss used the information was up to him. Oliver was just supposed to gather information; he didn't decide how to use it. He had known the Boss long enough to avoid offering uncalled for suggestions, no matter how sound the reasoning.

The Boss was crafty and seemed to be always prepared. Oliver had seen him destroy other men with both his fists and his skill with a gun. The Boss was also a prima donna and was always immaculately dressed, always wearing a jacket regardless of the heat. He was one of those that never seemed to sweat. Oliver knew the Boss carried holstered matching hip guns, a knife, and Oliver even suspected he carried a hideout gun up his sleeve. He noticed the Boss was very careful about how he carried his right arm, not to mention the unusual lump in his coat sleeve. It had to be a hideout gun and it was something to keep in mind.

The night had proven very profitable for Oliver. He was very pleased with his booty and mentally patted himself on the back. The dead Whip had donated a new knife and sheath as well as a decent bolo tie made of silver and turquoise, which Oliver planned on using at more formal gatherings. The Whip had also contributed $47 dollars and change, which would partially make up for the money from the hunter the Boss was making Oliver return. He had checked for a money belt just in case but he was disappointed. Oliver was also now sporting a new belt for his pants, a neckerchief, a tobacco pouch and a coin poke. The Whip was a treasure trove, but the most important possession Oliver carried back was valuable information, information he hoped would completely redeem himself to his Boss.

Once he had distanced himself from the stagecoach and the camp, he mounted his horse, but due to the darkness of the night he could only slow trot back to the camp. It wasn't far but at this rate it would take him a good two hours. The last thing he needed was to lame up his horse so he rode cautiously. He wanted to get back for Rodrigo was cooking dinner, and Oliver wanted his share. Rodrigo could cook – and evidenced by his size, he could eat as well!

Then Rory saw a dark spot in the dust a few yards from where Vivian had been. He even risked lighting a match to inspect it but it wasn't blood as he originally thought, instead it was the dainty red lace handkerchief Vivian had used during the ride. It had been ground into the dirt and Rory had mistaken it for a pool of blood. He picked it up and shook the dirt out of it. It still smelled lightly of the toilet water Vivian had used on the drive. He then pocketed the handkerchief, believing Vivian would surely want it back.

Rory's mind was racing, but he wasn't yet willing to make the assumption his fear-filled mind was becoming fixed upon. Rory thought he best check around the stagecoach again and see if Vivian had gone for some food or water following the battle. No Vivian. His concern for her safety was building, and he was beginning to believe the worst. He decided to go back and check out her station one more time before he went and shared his concerns with Lowe.

Back at her station Rory peaked around the rocks. He didn't see anybody alive or dead. He was about to go back and ask Lowe what he had seen and heard when he saw a dark shape about fifty feet in front of a perimeter rock and nestled next to a smaller rock. Whether it was safe or not, Rory had to know about Vivian, so slipping Vivian's gun into his belt and keeping low to the ground he carefully wound around the smaller rocks and covered the distance in seconds. As he approached, Rory could tell the dark shape was indeed a body. His worst fears realized.

His heart sank as he got closer but just as quickly he realized the body was not Vivian's but was that of a man. The man was very dead, and the shot that had taken his life was

# SEVEN

Night was fast approaching but the moon hadn't made an appearance yet and so the stars seemed to shine twice as bright in the crisp desert air. Foré and Vivian were talking when Rory approached them to issue them weapons.

Thinking Vivian would prefer the rifle, her response surprised him. 'It doesn't matter,' she said, 'I am proficient with either.' Seeing Foré's shocked expression and Rory's doubtful one, she explained that her uncle had taught her the use of guns since he had become her guardian.

'My uncle told me that the only person anyone can really depend upon for protection was themselves. Having lost both my parents, I vowed never to be at anyone's mercy again. I have practiced, even while at boarding school, where I raised quite a few eyebrows. I can assure you I can hit my target with either weapon. In fact,' she continued with an air that Rory wasn't sure was arrogance or confidence, 'I have my own pistol,' which she proudly produced from her handbag. It was a Moore .32 caliber Teatfire Revolver with a two-inch barrel, which she handed to Rory for his inspection. Rory was impressed and then handed it to Foré, who looked ashen.

'Nice piece,' Rory said admiringly, while Foré, to his credit, was calmly and carefully inspecting the tiny revolver. 'I carry a similar one as my back-up.'

'A back-up?' Vivian asked. 'You mean you carry one like this and still have your Colts?'

'Just being prepared,' Rory sheepishly said. As soon as he said it, Rory realized he was becoming too comfortable with Vivian as to reveal his secrets. He really didn't know anything about her other than what she shared only a few hours ago. He as quickly dismissed his concerns as she was young, beautiful and had a disarming manner about her that men responded too. Rory was smitten.

'So,' Vivian asked, 'which gun do I get? You can't expect me to repel enemies at distance with just my .32.'

'Is there a gun you would prefer?'

'Owing to Mr Foré's lack of experience, it would probably be better for him to have the rifle, as it takes less practice to become proficient,' Vivian responded in a matter of fact manner.

'Is that okay with you Foré?' Rory asked.

Foré swallowed, handed Vivian her small revolver back and reached out for the rifle. 'Do you really think we need shoot someone?' he asked with significant trepidation.

'I hope not, but we had best be prepared,' Rory responded as he handed Vivian a large Army Colt and the means to reload it. He then handed Foré his rifle. 'This is a Henry repeater so, so…' Looking at Foré's blank fleshy face, Rory continued, 'Perhaps Vivian will instruct you on its operation while I walk the perimeter.'

Rory had two reasons for having Vivian teach Foré about his rifle. He didn't have the time or patience to teach Foré, and he wanted to see if Vivian was as familiar with firearms as she implied. 'We'll position ourselves at different places, and each will be responsible for their approach. We'll take turns staying awake. I'll be back to fill you both in before it gets too late.'

Rory walked away a bit, then turned back to watch Vivian give instruction. He could tell Vivian knew her weapons as she took the rifle from Foré, then levered the action and inspected the chamber. She blew it out, then levered it closed. She swung it to her shoulder and aimed down the barrel. She then proceeded to show Foré how to load, aim, practice dry shoot, lever the next bullet and repeat the procedure several times.

After watching for a moment, Rory went to go find Lowe. Though Vivian did seemed familiar with weapons, Rory had his concerns. Familiarity is one thing, and Vivian seemed very familiar, even confident – but for all her bravado, shooting a person was a whole lot different than shooting a practice target, and it wasn't just that the target might be shooting back, but the idea of ending a human life. Killing was something few people grew accustomed to, which Rory believed was still a good thing. He wondered whether Vivian was really up to the task.

Funny, but Rory didn't feel the same apprehension with Foré. That Foré was out of his element and that he was scared was obvious, but Foré seemed to Rory to be someone who would stand their ground, whether fearful or not. He had no doubt Foré would use his ammunition because it was the right thing to do. He would shoulder his burden in defense of his fellows. If they got into a gunfight Foré might soil himself, but Rory believed he would be shooting in the process.

The more Rory worked and spoke with Foré, the more the big man impressed him. He wasn't a Westerner, but Rory could tell he had the makings. He originally thought it good that Foré was traveling on to California, but now he wasn't so sure.

It took a special kind of person to come and try to eke a living out of the West because the West was unforgiving to the uneducated and inexperienced, and the West usually didn't offer a learning curve. The more you survived, the better your chances. His gut told him Foré had what it took...if he survived. He almost laughed out loud after thinking of gut and Foré in the same sentence. Anyway, Rory would have to assess Foré again after this experience.

'So you think we are ready for the night?' Lowe asked after walking up to Rory, disturbing his reverie.

'Yea, I think so. We're in a protective enclosure with limited access. All approaches are covered. We have sufficient fire power and ammunition,' Rory shared. 'Yea, I think we'll be okay. But I don't want Vivian and Foré to be next to each other. So, do you want the left or right front?'

'I take the right center,' Lowe said.

'Okay, I'll take the left and the first watch. It's almost dark and close to seven o'clock. I think three hours per watch will work. I'll let the others know. I think if they're going try anything it'll be during the first watch or the third, so you should take the third.'

'Sounds good,' Lowe said.

'Try to get some shut eye because I think the third shift will be the most difficult.'

'You're right about that,' Lowe said. After a second he added, 'You think Vivian and Foré are up to this?'

'I guess we're going to find out. Vivian will spell you around four o'clock.'

Lowe turned to go, but stopped mid-step. He turned back to Rory and said, 'You're young, but did you fight in the war?'

'Why do you ask?'

'Oh, you seem pretty savvy for being so young,' Lowe replied.

After a pause Rory responded, 'I was going to, but my Pa and I had a row over it. I left home because of it, but I never joined. How about you?'

'Nah. I got my sympathies, but I'm not willing to die for them,' Lowe said.

Rory nodded in understanding then said, 'There's some food in the stagecoach. Get a bite before you turn in.'

As Lowe walked away, Rory watched him first go to the coach and get some bread and cheese before heading to his position. After Lowe sat down and began eating, Rory considered it unfortunate that he would have to deal with Lowe when this was all over, but he had a job to do. He turned and walked toward Vivian and Foré.

Vivian was sitting on a rock watching Foré practice with the rifle in the darkness. Rory walked up and first commended Foré, 'Looks like you're getting a handle on that rifle.'

'*Oui.* Vivian is being good teacher,' Foré responded.

'It not only takes a good teacher but also a bright student,' Vivian responded with equal enthusiasm.

'Well, good job to both of you, but now I think you two need to turn in. I'll be taking the right front position and Lowe the front left. Foré, you'll be on my right and Vivian will be on Lowe's left. I'll be taking the first watch, followed by you, Foré, then Lowe and finally you, Vivian. Each shift will be about three hours. Don't move around, just stay alert. Hopefully all this is unnecessary, but we have to be prepared.'

'And if someone is come when my watch?' Foré asked.

'Raise an alarm. I think we'll all be sleeping lightly and it won't take much to alert the rest of us.'

'I am scared, much scared for death, but I do my part,' Foré said, his faulting English and thick accent accentuated by his fear.

'I know you will,' Rory said, patting him on his large, fleshy arm. 'Fear is not the opposite of courage,' he said, 'cowardice is.'

'I will not let all down,' Foré said as he indicated toward Vivian and even Lowe with his hand.

'You will do fine. We are all afraid at times. It is what we do with our fear that determines who we really are. I trust you. Now get some food and turn in. You will spell me at eleven, which is about four hours from now'.

After Foré left, Rory asked Vivian, 'How about you? You ready?'

'I think so,' Vivian said quietly.

'You surprised me with your knowledge of firearms,' Rory said.

'And you surprised me by your heroism and leadership,' Vivian said. 'Just look at Mr Foré. He seems determined to fight and die if need be.'

'Heroism?' Rory asked with a smirk.

'Yes, heroism,' Vivian said with conviction. 'You risked your life when you saved us in the stagecoach, and now you are organizing our defenses. If we make it through all this it will be mainly because of you.' And with that, she rose up on her tip toes and pressing herself against him, kissed Rory's cheek.

Luckily for Rory it was dark as he was instantly and embarrassingly blushing. He was a blusher, and once it started, any attention it brought only intensified the effect. He had always considered his blushing a curse, especially when a young lady friend back in Washington described it as being cute. He could think of a number of other descriptive words that were more manly then cute. Cute was how you described a puppy, not a federal secret service agent. Blushing was one of Rory's least favorite subjects.

Rory knew Vivian couldn't see him blushing because of the darkness, so he decided to try and ignore the kiss, but unfortunately he stuttered in his response, '...Uh, ...um, ... okay.'

As soon as the comment came out of his mouth Rory could have kicked himself. Women seem to instinctively know when they make a man uncomfortable, and Vivian, being a young and beautiful woman, seemed very aware she was making him self-conscious.

Rory believed this was a game that most, if not all women play, at least from his limited experience. It seemed to Rory that women purposely test the waters of male nature and see if they can solicit a response. He suddenly realized this game was similar to the new British sport of fly fishing, which Rory had recently experimented with and enjoyed immensely. The key to fly fishing was to lure the fish with a fake fly, compelling it to rise and strike. This analogy unfortunately compelled Rory to think of himself as the fish, and he found that very disconcerting. That he might be a helpless and thrashing fish trying to free itself from a tenacious hook was truly horrifying, especially considering the possible future of the fish – gutted, buttered and fried. With that metaphor now locked in his mind, his passion for fly fishing seemed somehow less gratifying, and it made him even more wary of alluring women.

Though his experience with women was limited, he had still seen the game played many, many times. In his mind it almost seemed like playing the game was how some women measured their worth. He truly believed that women want to be wanted, and they want to see the effect they have on men whether they are truly interested in the man they are focused upon or not – tempting and luring with the promise of a reward, sometimes sincerely and sometimes not. The problem with this game was that it moves both participants forward to a possible conclusion, which in truth, neither might actually want. Unfortunately Rory's seeming hesitancy seemed to inspire Vivian's response as she then pulled his arm to her and holding tightly to him, led him to her assigned spot.

It was dark, and Rory couldn't see Foré or Lowe, but his self-consciousness caused him to believe they were watching his discomfort. Rory wondered whether Vivian was doing this just to see whether, like a fish, he would rise and strike. Did the kiss even mean anything to her, or was it just a lure? Was he merely the fish in her game, or was she actually interested in him? If by chance she was truly interested in him, how was he to know? Rather than play along, he did what his mother had taught him from the Good Book, 'gird up your loins!' He would keep Vivian and her womanly wiles at arms' length. This he realized would be harder than he thought, as even now she was pressing his arm against her chest as they walked to her assigned area. It was obvious by his response to Vivian's attentions, regardless whether she was serious or not, that he was an ill-prepared participant in the game.

'So this is my post?' Vivian asked Rory when they arrived at the parameter of the rocks. 'I am to defend it to the death?' she said with a mocking seriousness.

'Yes,' Rory responded uncomfortably, trying not to take the bait. 'It'll be easy to defend as you have rock walls to your left and behind you, and Lowe will be on your right.' He waited for Vivian to release his arm so he could go to his own post, but she held on and so he waited, trying to focus on anything but Vivian.

'So you think someone is going to attack us?' Vivian asked, looking up into his face.

'I don't know,' he said, 'but we need to be prepared for whatever comes.'

After an uncomfortable, silent minute Vivian finally did let go of Rory's arm, then asked with a seriousness she had thus far kept out of her voice, 'You are asking me to shoot someone tonight?'

'Maybe. I only know someone shot the Whip, and the only reason for that was the hope that we would crash. Whoever shot the Whip wants something pretty badly, and they are willing to kill us to get it.'

'That poor man,' Vivian said. 'The Whip, I mean. I didn't even know his name.'

'His name was Clarence Joyce, but he liked being called the Whip and with a name like Clarence, I can understand why. As far as being shot, I doubt he even knew what hit him. It was a large caliber bullet and it not only went through him, it passed through the cabin, barely missing you and Foré before splintering Lowe's rifle stock he had stored in the boot. In my opinion, we are lucky to be alive, and you twice over. You could have been killed by the bullet, and then again when the stagecoach almost went over the side of the road. I usually don't hold with luck, but right now we are riding high. We've been very, very lucky.'

Though he often attributed positive outcomes to Lady Luck, Rory was not one to trust in her. He had been blessed by her in the past, but he really believed that luck was more likely brought about because of thorough preparation – though that belief couldn't always explain outcomes. There have been times when he had fully prepared and yet nothing had worked out right. And on the other hand, he had flown by the seat of his pants and could do no wrong. In his experience, Lady Luck was fickle, which might explain why luck in general was referred to as a Lady. As Lady Luck was fickle, he wasn't about to make her his mistress.

'I just know I was so scared,' Vivian said wrapping her arms around herself as if to reassure herself. Holding on to the large pistol while she made the motion was almost comical, but Rory wasn't going to disrupt the serious tone of their conversation. He wanted Vivian to understand that this could be a life or death situation, and humor had no place in their preparations right now.

'Well, they obviously didn't get what they wanted, so I assume they will try again and we had better be ready,' Rory said. Then after a second he asked, 'What do you think of your gun?'

Vivian unwrapped her arms and lifted the large Army Colt with both hands, pretending to sight down the barrel, 'I'm ready.'

'That's a lot of gun. You sure you can handle it?'

'Uh... I think so.'

Rory heard Vivian hesitate when referring to her weapon, and asked her, 'You ever shoot at a live target?'

'No,' she said, her voice seemed hesitant, lacking the confidence she had exhibited previously. 'Nothing alive, and especially not a human being. Does it show that much?' she asked. 'Before, I was just trying to be brave so as not to stress Mr Foré.'

'That doesn't matter. When the shooting starts you just focus on the fact that whoever is attacking has already tried to kill you and they are trying to do so again. You need to make up your mind that you are shooting to kill, for they seem intent on doing the same.'

'I'm not sure I can do that,' she said with a catch in her voice. 'I don't know if I can kill someone.'

'Well, we are counting on you to protect this flank,' Rory said as he faced her and placed his hands on her shoulders. 'If you don't think you can kill someone to protect yourself, then consider protecting the rest of us. We need you here to cover this side. We are counting on you.'

'I'll try,' she said.

'You'll do fine. You are just like Foré – you have strength you don't even know you have. I'm not worried,' Rory said. 'You will do what needs to be done.'

'All right,' Vivian said. 'If you say so,' her voice trailing off almost to a whisper, which Rory found disturbingly seductive.

Was she really insecure, Rory wondered, or was she just playing him again? Pushing the thought aside he knew it was now up to her. 'I believe in you, Vivian,' he said. 'Now try to get some sleep. You will have the last watch before daylight.'

As he walked away, leaving her standing and staring after him, Rory decided Vivian was an enigma. One minute she was flirty and confident, the next she was insecure. One minute she is teaching how to use a rifle, and the next she is unsure whether she can use a gun to defend her own life. One minute she is kissing him and holding him close, and the next she, she... When it came to women, Rory decided he was just a helpless fish.

# EIGHT

It was during the second watch under the smallest of the silver moon. Foré was on guard. He was sitting with his back against the rocks at his post when he heard the sound. It was just a whisper but it wasn't what he had accustomed himself to hearing during his watch. The sound perked him right up, and any drowsiness he was experiencing vanished. It sounded like a soft buffing sound, like shifting sand or cloth lightly scuffing rock. He lifted his rifle. Was that a shadow moving out there? Should he call out and alert his friends? What if he was wrong? Should he investigate the sound himself? Questions, fear and sweat were his response. He might be wrong and embarrass himself, but he knew the risks and Rory had made it clear what had to be done. He yelled, 'Someone is here!'

As soon as Foré raised the alarm there was a loud bang and he felt a searing pain in his side. But he had seen the flash of light, and through the pain and suddenness of the shot, he still raised his rifle and squeezed off a shot just as he had been taught.

Immediately there was shouting and frantic activity. There was another bang and a loud whoosh followed by a blinding light as the gunpowder Lowe had placed in the fire pile ignited. The defenders knew not to look at the light, but the attackers were instantly blinded by the flash – and not only blinded, but revealed to the defenders, who immediately began firing.

Rory had heard Foré's alarm and was instantly awake. He came off the ground quickly and crouched behind a rock looking for a target. He heard Lowe moving to the fire and was pleased to see the effects of the blinding light when the powder ignited and the enemy was revealed. Whereas before there was just shouting and chaos, now there was gunfire, and mostly from the defenders.

Once the gunpowder had burned off, the only remaining light was the subdued flicker of the tiny fire now burning the limited brushwood gathered earlier by Vivian and Foré. Rory could see Lowe firing and Vivian, poised, holding the big Colt with both hands and aiming down the barrel, assuming she was making each shot count. Foré was lying on the ground on his stomach but he was also firing.

A bullet suddenly struck the rock Rory was using as a shield and then whined off into the darkness, knocking his hat off in the process. The rocks were of sandstone, and the bullet spattered rock debris on to the side of Rory's head. That was close, and he knew he was bleeding from a few small cuts, but he was thankful he hadn't been facing the spattering of rock or he might have lost an eye. He fired at the startled face of a man who was rushing the parameter, and was pleased to see him go down. He emptied his right-side gun then drew his other one, and using a border shift, never missed a beat. He even holstered the empty gun while taking a bead on a man running toward Foré's position. The gun bucked in his hand and the running man spun and dropped. But just as quickly the man was up and running in retreat. Rory was pretty sure he had clipped him, but the wound didn't seem serious as the man was still able to beat it back into the darkness.

Now it was total chaos. There was gunfire all around him, but as far as Rory could tell the attackers hadn't made it into their camp. He heard shouting and cursing mixed with the sounds of running feet and men exerting themselves. The attackers were mostly using hand guns on the run as it appeared they were trying to charge into the camp. He believed he had killed one and wounded another, and was confident Lowe would get one, if not more. The commotion seemed to last for hours, but in fact lasted just a few moments. During the din Rory heard someone outside the parameter whistle loudly, and as quickly as the attack began, it was over, the shadows scattering like roaches.

'Everybody stay down,' Rory shouted into the now silent night. The silence was eerie, as just moments before the air had been alive with the sounds of death. The gunpowder had ignited the little amount of brush that Vivian and Foré had collected, but it was now yielding very little light and soon the small flame went out, leaving only smoldering coals and a lot of smoke. It was too dark to really see anything, but Rory could make out a couple of dark mounds which he assumed were bodies. It had been a costly attack for the enemy, with at least two men down.

'Everybody okay?' Rory called out.

'Okay,' came back Lowe.

'Vivian?'

After some hesitation Rory heard a muffled 'Okay'. Her voice didn't sound right, but Rory figured she was still scared, for just seconds ago, death had raged. He couldn't blame her as they had just been attacked in the darkness and men were dead, perhaps even some of their own team. Whoever these men were, they were bold and determined. He had been through gun battles before and even he was a little apprehensive about this confrontation. One thing he was sure of, now that they had lost men, they would force the issue until they got what they came for. To be safe, he decided he would go check on Vivian, if for anything just to buoy up her confidence.

'Foré?' There was no answer, so Rory called out again, 'Foré?'

'I am shot!' Foré responded weakly.

'Stay down, I'm coming over,' Rory responded.

Looking around and not seeing any movement, Rory called to Lowe, 'Lowe, you see anything out there? Foré has been hit and I need to go check him out.'

'No. It looks clear, but these guys are snakes,' Lowe responded. 'You can chance it if you want, but I think they're still around.'

'Thanks Lowe. If you see a movement or a flash, you know what to do!'

'My pleasure.'

Rory needed to get to Vivian, but Foré was injured and became his first priority. He looked around as best as he could, but it was too dark to see whether the attackers had completely left or were still around just waiting for a target. Figuring he simply had to take his chances, he kept low to the ground and dashed over to where he believed Foré was. When he was nearing Foré a bullet clipped the ground, kicking up dust and barely missing him. Rory was pleased to hear Lowe respond with a shot of his own.

Rory found Foré sitting up with his hand holding his filthy bandanna against his side. Rory knelt beside him to assess the damage.

'It hurts, my friend,' Foré said, 'but I don't think it serious.'

Even in the splintered moonlight, Rory could see the blood squeezing between Foré's fingers. Rory pulled Foré's hand back and inspected the wound as best he could in the limited light. Foré was right: the bullet had just clipped his side, and luckily for him his side was of ample dimensions and the bullet had passed cleanly.

'It is bleeding, but you'll be okay,' Rory said, trying to reassure Foré. 'Do just what you are doing, hold it tight against the wound.'

'I'm big man with plenty space to get shoot,' Foré said, trying to make light of his wound, but his accent was forced with each grimace of pain.

'You did good,' Rory said. 'You alerted us in time, and reduced their numbers by at least one,' he said, pointing to a crumpled figure about twenty feet away.

'He is dead?'

'I haven't checked him, but from the way he is lying there, he probably is,' Rory said. 'You okay with that?'

'He was run toward me,' Foré said. Then speaking quieter he said, 'I remember his face look. It still in my mind.'

'Unfortunately that is something you never forget, but just remember he was going to kill you.' Seeing Foré's concern, Rory grabbed Foré by his big shoulders and said to his face, 'You did good Foré, I am glad you are with us.'

Foré smiled at the compliment, then asked, 'You think they try again?'

'Well, they still didn't get what they came for, thanks to you,' Rory said, as he pulled a bandanna from his own pocket. 'They might try again tonight, but I don't think so. They lost too many men.' Then changing the subject he asked, 'You got any spirits with you?'

'I am French! Of course I have,' Foré said, and he reached inside his breast pocket and produced a small flask which he opened, took a quick pull and then handed the open container to Rory.

'This is going to hurt, but the sooner we clean the wound the better the chances of eliminating any infection,' Rory said as he poured a small amount of the alcohol into the wound, and then a bit on to his bandanna to begin wiping away the blood.

'Oh, is waste,' Foré lamented through clenched teeth as the alcohol touched the open and raw wound.

'This will only be a temporary fix until we can actually see what we are doing, then we can bandage you properly,' Rory said, grabbing and squeezing Foré's arm to reassure him. 'Just keep pressure until it stops bleeding and avoid too much motion. I'll get you some water, so just relax and sleep if you can.'

'Thank you, my friend,' Foré said, the sincerity in his voice unmistakable.

'You did good tonight, Foré,' Rory said, as he hurried to the stagecoach to get a canteen. Getting to the coach was easy, as the path was mostly sheltered. The coach was okay, but one of the horses was down. Must have been a wild shot or a ricochet. This was unfortunate, as it limited their options for escape, but at least they now had more food. As soon as it was light he would have to butcher the horse and save the best cuts, possibly make some jerky out of it.

Getting a canteen, Rory also got some cheese to give to Foré. As he was returning to him, he concluded that he had definitely been wrong about Foré. Even though he seemed soft, Foré had the makings of a solid western man and he belonged here. Rory determined he would share this thought with Foré once they were out of danger.

After giving Foré the water and cheese, and once he was confident that Foré was okay, Rory called to Lowe that he was now going over to see to Vivian.

'I dusted the last muzzle flash so I think they will be more wary before exposing themselves,' Lowe said, with that hint of confidence Rory had detected earlier. Say what you will about Lowe, Rory thought, he was glad they were on the same side.

Keeping low to the ground, Rory scooted over to Vivian's area. Vivian's was a little further from Lowe than Foré's was from Rory. As he neared the area he quietly called out in an urgent whisper, 'Vivian, where are you?' There was no response. His first reaction was that she might have been killed but he dismissed that as her body would be lying in sight. Not seeing her brought him a measure of assurance. When he finally arrived at the rock Vivian was going to use for protection he found the area vacant. No Vivian.

'Vivian, where are you?' Rory whispered as loudly as he felt was safe. He was answered by silence, the worst kind of silence that can follow a gunfight. The light was limited, but Rory searched the area and Vivian was nowhere to be found. He did find the large pistol Vivian was using and the earth looked like it had been churned up some. Had there been a struggle? He checked the loads and found the pistol had been shot four times. There was no blood that he could see, so at least she wasn't injured.

well placed, right between the eyes. The heavy slug from the Colt used by Vivian had done its job and Rory doubted the man even knew he had been hit. Vivian had been truthful all right. She could use a weapon, and it seemed she was totally unmoved by killing. Rory looked at the hole in the man's face. Even he questioned whether he could have shot so cleanly from so far and in the dark. Luck? Not likely, Rory decided. When it came to killing, Vivian was more than she represented. During a fight, she was a cold customer. Rory quickly looked around and found nothing else. Swearing under his breath, he hurried back to Vivian's spot and then over to Lowe.

'Vivian is gone,' Rory told Lowe as soon as he was within whispering distance.

'What?' Lowe asked.

'I said, Vivian is gone!'

'Did you check back at the stagecoach?'

'I did, and I thoroughly checked her area. She is gone. Did you hear anything?' Rory asked Lowe.

'In the beginning, I heard her shoot but during the thick of the fight, I guess I lost track of her.'

'Well, I found her gun and her handkerchief. I originally thought the handkerchief was blood but as I got closer I realized what it was. I did notice that the ground around her area was pretty scuffed up. I think they took her.'

'Kidnapped? Lowe asked incredulously. 'You think she was kidnapped?'

'What else could it be?' Rory asked.

'The ground looked like there was a struggle?'

'As far as I could see in this light it looked pretty churned up,' Rory said. 'I think she must have put up quite a fight, but she is gone.'

'I can't believe I didn't see or hear anything,' Lowe said, pounding his fist on his thigh. 'I wonder if she was knocked out and dragged off. Maybe that is why I didn't hear anything.'

'If that is true, we will see the drag marks in the dirt,' Rory said. 'I think Vivian's got sand and I doubt she would have gone willingly. When it is light we can inspect the area more closely.'

'I can't get over the idea they snatched her, and right under my nose!' Lowe said angrily.

'Don't beat yourself up over this. We had our hands full in that fight. And if the assault was just a diversion to get Vivian, then it was a painful one. I believe they lost at least four men and I know I dusted at least one.

'I know I got at one and maybe more. Maybe clipped a few,' Lowe said with his confident air.

'What do you think they are up to? Kidnapping? What could they possibly want?' Rory asked, watching Lowe closely.

'Maybe they just wanted Vivian,' Lowe offered.

'Doesn't fit, as she would have been killed just like the rest of us in the crash. No, there is something we are missing here.'

'Yea, maybe, but what?' Lowe said.

Rory looked at Lowe incredulously. He believed Lowe knew darn well what these men were after. They wanted the same thing Rory wanted and would have to take from Lowe as soon as this situation was over and done with: the map of the gold mine. That Lowe was feigning innocence about this whole mess, and now that Foré was injured and Vivian was missing, the whole situation was eating at Rory. Finally Rory said, 'The only thing I can think is that they hope to trade her for something we have. The question bothering me is what do we have that they want?'

As if he hadn't even heard the question, Lowe said, 'Well, we are going to get her back, ain't we?'

'I think we need to try but I would imagine we will find out what they want come morning. If they kidnapped her and are holding her for ransom, I am sure they will let us know. Kidnappers usually have demands,' Rory said, then added, 'The fight was over at least two hours ago so they are probably already back at their camp arguing among themselves trying to figure out what went wrong, and what they are going to do.'

Suddenly a solitary shot resounded in the stillness of the night. Rory and Lowe looked at each other, Lowe with a questioning look and Rory with a very concerned look. The sound of the shot had come from a small caliber weapon, quite possibly Vivian's pistol. Rory wondered whether Vivian was now dead or had she just tried to kill someone else.

'You hear that?'

'Small caliber,' said Lowe. 'I figure about a mile distance.'

Rory nodded his head in agreement then shared, 'If Vivian had her purse with her, that could have been her .32. Did you know she kept a small revolver in her purse?'

The surprise on Lowe's face was absolute and genuine. 'Vivian kept a hog?'

'She sure did. It was only a .32 Teatfire revolver, but she showed it to me and Foré,' Rory said. 'She also implied she was proficient in its use.'

'You think that was hers?' Lowe asked.

'Could be. And if so, I think she is either dead or she just shot someone,' Rory responded. 'Of course she also might be trying to let us know where she is.'

'Well, I hope she didn't waste the shot,' Lowe said. 'They are bad men and deserve death.'

'Part of me hopes she wasted the shot and part hopes she didn't,' Rory said. 'They lost a lot of men over this and things might go ill for her if she killed or injured another of their group.'

'They wouldn't harm a woman,' Lowe said confidently. 'Even these low life's still respect women out here.'

'Yes, but they were willing to kill her in the attempted stagecoach crash. I don't think these men feel completely bound by the unwritten laws of the West,' Rory said. 'Right now, I think Vivian is merely a means to an end.'

'But if they kill her, they'll lose their bargaining chip.'

'I hope you are right.' Rory paused, then looked at Lowe and said, 'So you agree we have something they want, something they would be willing to bargain for Vivian?'

Lowe nodded his head. Rory let the silence drag on, hoping Lowe would finally come clean – and finally Lowe said, 'I think they want something I have.'

'What have you got that is so important?'

Lowe looked around, and after inclining his head to Rory, said, 'A map.'

'Just a map?' Rory asked.

'This ain't just any map,' Lowe said quietly and confidently. 'It is a very valuable map.'

Rory mimicked Lowe's confidential approach and asked quietly, 'A map of what?'

'You don't need to know, but believe me, it is an important map.'

Rory nodded as if he understood and respected Lowe's privacy. He felt awkward playing Lowe like he was. Lowe has always been up front with Rory, while Rory felt he wasn't being up front with Lowe, at least not totally. Like most in the West, Lowe may not have revealed everything he knew about something, but when it counted, like now, Lowe was true. According to the intelligence Rory had received for this assignment, Lowe was hired to do a simple job: he was to guard and deliver a map to someone, and Rory was sure that, typical of men in the West, Lowe was a man of his word. He had accepted money for a service and he would do his duty, as he saw it, come hell or high water. Rory was growing uneasy the more he learned about Lowe, that when the time came for him to take the map, Lowe wouldn't be inclined to surrender it.

'So what do you think we should do?' Lowe asked.

Lowe was a good ten years older than Rory's twenty-two years, but Rory found it interesting that Lowe, Foré and even Vivian seemed to look to him for leadership. Was it his assertiveness? He was no fence sitter, for sure, and once a decision was made he did his best to see it done. But what was he to do now? His boss would tell him to just get the map and get out, but that was not Rory's way. True, he had a job to do and that job didn't include looking out for others, but the West breeds a sense of responsibility. The cause might sometimes be skewed, but the convictions beneath the cause were founded upon right and wrong. If anything, the West was predictable.

Out West, a body was held accountable for his actions, even if those actions led to a hangman's noose. Everybody understood that, even the accused. Justice was expected by all and meted out quickly. This was one of those times when Rory knew his staying here and seeing this to a conclusion was the right thing to do. But now his job involved betraying a man with whom he had fought side by side, and now the two of them might be going to risk their lives to go rescue a woman, whom neither of them really knew but who was accepted as a partner. Lowe might not be an upstanding citizen according to eastern standards, but to Rory, Lowe was a solid westerner. This whole undercover business was beginning to go against Rory's grain.

'I don't think they will harm Vivian, and I am confident they will let us know what they expect in exchange for her,' Rory stated.

'Yup, I think you are right,' said Lowe.

'So how attached are you to this map, and how is it that they know you have it?' Rory asked.

'I was paid to deliver the map to an individual in California. Other than that, I don't know nothin.'

'Would you be willing to give up the map?'

'I would rather not,' Lowe said. 'I took money. I got to see this through.'

'And Vivian?'

'We'll get her back even if I got to kill every last one of those snakes!'

Watching Lowe and seeing the intensity in his face, Rory was convinced that Lowe would make good on his pledge, or die trying.

# NINE

The desert night was pristine. The stars were brilliant in the expansive cooling black with just a sliver of moon. The beauty should impress but the angry group that returned to the gathering place was totally unaware. Tempers were high and the anger in the air was tangible. The group had lost six men and two were wounded. The wounds were not severe, but the pain of the two wounded men only added fuel to the anger and frustration. It was obvious to the Boss that any additional frustration might lead to mutiny, which if it occurred, would lead to additional deaths. The Boss was ruthless and if his followers lost confidence in his ability to bring them riches, he was fully ready to shoot his way clear – but he still needed these men to help him achieve his goal.

The men dismounted and gathered around the fire that Ranger was resurrecting. Oliver carried the tied and unconscious Vivian and laid her down next to a rock by the small but growing fire. She was sporting an ugly welt where she had been struck to prevent her from fighting back.

With his smooth-talking southern aristocratic voice, the Boss said, 'Well, boys, that experience was most unfortunate. We lost valuable men.'

His comment immediately brought disgruntled mumbles from the rest of the group, 'Yea, we did!' Ranger said. 'They cut us in half.'

'I thought you said they was tinhorns!' Casper said, who was nursing a small flesh wound in his left arm.

'It was only three men and a woman,' Ranger said in disgust.

'They had it planned. The fire and all. We didn't have a chance,' Mason said.

'Lucky for us the Boss had us snatch the woman,' Oliver said.

'Yea, what about that? I don't cotton on to abusing womenfolk,' Mason said.

'You said this was supposed to be easy money!' Roscoe said.

'And you will get your money,' the Boss said. 'And much more than you would have earned working cows.'

'We lost six good men. Right now, working cows don't sound that bad,' Casper said.

'I know we lost men,' the Boss replied, purposefully without using the word 'good', 'and I feel their loss as much as you.'

'I doubt that. I have known some of these men for years,' Mason said. 'What you claim as a loss, I say was a friend of twenty years!'

'So just what are you saying?' the Boss asked, with a growing edge in his voice. 'What do you expect?' he said, looking around at the angry faces flickering in the light of the campfire. When no one said anything, the Boss pressed the point, 'Any of you can leave anytime you want. We'll just split up your share.'

'Just saying, your plans was bad,' Mason said, as he straightened up from the fire and faced the Boss. 'You said the stagecoach would crash, it didn't. You said we could charge their camp, and being tinhorns they would panic and scatter, and they didn't.' As he spoke, the Boss was aware that a few of the crew were nodding their heads in agreement. 'You promised us lots of money, but all we got to show for our work so far... is dead friends.'

Instantly the group was divided. Obviously the Boss had his supporters, but the unspoken had been spoken and it was now out in the open for debate. Coupled with the emotional losses, the complaints grew in intensity and unity. The Boss could sense his diminishing authority. Mason was becoming disruptive and may need to be dealt with. The Boss needed to restore his authority, and quickly. He had tried using persuasive reasoning to quell the mistrust, then he had appealed to their greed, but he knew in the back of his mind that if he could not restore his authority, he would have to use his guns.

Thinking he could still overcome his detractors with one last argument, the Boss waved his hand for quiet, then said, 'We did not return empty-handed. We have a valuable hostage. In case our attack didn't work, I had an alternative plan, to abduct the woman. She is our hostage, and will guarantee we get what we came for!'

'A hostage?' asked Mason.

'The woman?' asked Ranger with disgust.

The Boss instantly realized he had again misjudged his gang in announcing his alternative plan, as the next words from Mason were, 'I don't know how things is back in the south where you come from, but out here, we don't cotton on to abusing womenfolk!'

The Boss's eyes narrowed, and taking a step closer to Mason he said, 'True, and if the men from the stagecoach feel the same way as you, then they will gladly make an exchange.' The Boss was growing irritated that he was now having to justify his actions. Just who were these men, anyway? They were just stupid guns for hire. The lowest of the low. The Boss was of old southern aristocracy, and he believed these men were lucky even to have someone of his standing to lead them.

The Boss, born Gerald Remington Harrison III, was a disenfranchised southern gentleman of the distinguished Charleston Harrisons of South Carolina. His widowed father fervently believed in the resolution the South Carolina General Assembly passed on 9 November 1860, that the election of Abraham Lincoln as US President was 'a hostile act'! As one of the first of the 169 delegates elected to attend the Convention of the People of South Carolina, and one of the loudest advocates of succession, the senior Harrison had offered his fortune to support South Carolina's cause.

Gerald did not possess his father's political fervor, and was dismayed when his father was later commissioned an officer in the Confederate Army. His dismay turned to horror when his father informed him that his inheritance had been legally dedicated to supporting South Carolina's war effort and the Confederacy. At that point in his life, Gerald was a well educated, dashing and, up until that point, wealthy twenty-four-year-old bachelor, sought after by many southern belles and their mothers. He fostered this standing, and at first even gloried in the attention his father was attracting with his powerful declarations. Unfortunately for the young Gerald, the Civil War popped this protective bubble of self-importance, and he soon found himself penniless and disinherited.

Upon his father's insistence, Gerald had enlisted in the Confederate cause and for a while he relished the attention he received when he attended the final balls before the war in his dashing and carefully tailored uniform. What Gerald hadn't counted upon was that he would ultimately be expected to actually fight a war, a war he didn't understand, and for a state he didn't particularly care about. As far as he was concerned, his priorities and his future had already been decreed – and then his father's political fervor had ruined everything. He didn't even feel sadness at the notification of his father's death at the First Battle of Kernstown.

Gerald's lackluster military career came to a dramatic conclusion during his first enemy engagement at the Battle of Port Royal. For the first time, the young Gerald realized war didn't fit in with his plans. He witnessed, up close, the dead and injured and realized he likewise could be maimed or even killed. So as soon as he could, he slipped away, shedding his fancy uniform as soon as opportunity presented itself at a clothesline outside Charleston.

Gerald couldn't go home because it no longer existed, and with no money, he went deeper south, using his genteel manner to take advantage of unsuspecting women for his support. He was finally found out and challenged by his current patron's young son to a dual. With his superb aristocratic training with weapons, he easily killed the boy, took what money he had accumulated and what valuables he could load in his pockets from the home of his final patron, and headed further south. Now wanted for robbery and possibly murder, Gerald had moved from place to place in a generally southern direction, using his skills with cards, guns and the occasional robbery to support himself. But with his every move, he vowed he would somehow recover his inheritance and live the life he believed he deserved.

Almost one year to the date of his desertion from the Confederate Army, Gerald unexpectedly found himself down in New Orleans in a serious card game with a gentleman wearing the uniform of a Confederate colonel. The game grew deadly when the Colonel was unable to make good on his debts. In the South, honor was paramount and welching on debts was unthinkable. After a show of good will, Gerald graciously and publicly allowed the Colonel to provide an IOU.

When the inebriated Colonel left the saloon, Gerald slipped out unobserved and followed the weaving soldier. When away from the public he forced the Colonel into an abandoned warehouse on a waterway and proceeded to beat the man to make good on his debt. When the man was not forthcoming with cash, the beating quickly escalated into torture as an outlet for Gerald's frustration. Colonel Franks finally broke and offered information he hoped would save his life. Through his mangled lips he informed Gerald of the presence of a map, the golden hope of the Confederacy.

Gerald's mind went berserk at the possibilities! Gold? A mine? He had heard of the vast gold accumulated by the Spanish. This could be the answer to all his problems. A gold mine, enough gold to help fund the Confederate cause, the Colonel said. Why, that could be... could be... millions of dollars! More money than he could even dream of. With this information, he could return to his estates and expand his holdings way beyond his father's. Why, he could buy a whole county, maybe even a state. Caught up in the fervor of fantasy he thought that if the money was to be used to support the Confederacy, it might be enough money to buy a country! He could become royalty, a king!

Gerald had to get all the information he could. This was just the opportunity he had been waiting for. Finally he could return with his head held high. He need no longer worry about the law as he would have enough money to own the law. He needed every bit of information the Colonel could provide. He needed that map. No, he needed the mine. He needed the gold!

As exciting as the thought was, Gerald was a lazy person and didn't have the capital or the willingness to actually mine the gold. He also wasn't about to share his new-found fortune with any greedy investors. After pausing to catch his breath, Gerald realized that he didn't actually need the gold. He decided to let the Confederacy mine the gold; they were planning on doing that anyway. Instead, he would simply obtain and sell the map to the Confederacy. He was confident he would be handsomely paid for the map. So, maybe not royalty, but he could still buy a state!

After giving up all the information he possessed, Colonel Franks conveniently died. Gerald quickly dumped the weighted-down body into the nearest bayou to prevent anyone else knowing what he had obtained. Now armed with the precious secret, Gerald headed west to secure what he believed would finally bring him restoration!

Gerald made good use of his time developing his plans, going west to Utah and contacting and securing the fifteen men he believed he would need. He knew these men wouldn't be high caliber, but he wanted to ensure his success, and so he figured fifteen men would allow for the inevitable loss any adventure such as this would require. He had played plenty of chess and knew the value of pawns.

The number of men he expected to enlist would require his buying more supplies for the three-day project, but he knew he would recoup his investment many times over. Once he had convinced and hired Oliver, the rest of the men came easily. Obviously Oliver had connections with the lower class.

Gerald had some trouble getting his sniper, but in time everything fell into place. And now, here he was, the Boss, and his precious map was within his grasp. It was so close he could see the glittering gold in his mind's eye – but now his whole plan was at risk. His gang, men he considered to be the lowest form of humanity, were standing on *principle*, of all things. Gerald doubted they had principles, or even knew what principles were. His entire plan, his re-emergence as a southern gentleman, was at risk because of what he considered to be an outmoded and meaningless act of chivalry.

To Gerald, chivalry was overrated. He believed one needed money to be truly chivalrous. Who would have thought these smelly outlaws would have a code of conduct when it came to women. Gerald looked at women merely as a means to an end, a chattel of sorts, the currency of advancement in a civilized society. With Vivian he had the currency to buy his future, and he wasn't about to allow anyone, especially these parasitic outlaws, to jeopardize all he had worked for. He was Gerald Remington Harrison III of the Charleston Harrisons of South Carolina! He was their Boss. He was in charge – and now these men were questioning his principles!

'We true Westerners do not molest womenfolk,' Mason re-emphasized. The dig regarding being a true Westerner was not lost upon any of the remaining gang, and especially the Boss.

A quick scan of the faces let the Boss know that the group was split. No doubt most of the men felt the same on principle, but not all were willing to jeopardize their paycheck. Obviously this was a very touchy subject out west and one the Boss intended to ignore, but he couldn't help but wonder why. Was it because there were fewer women than men and scarcity equals value? That made sense to the Boss, as throughout history women were often bought and sold. Was it some sort of primitive drive to protect the means of adding members to the tribe? Maybe it was all just carnality. Whatever the reason, the Boss pushed his thoughts aside and focused his attention and direction. He had a woman of value, and he wasn't going to let anyone jeopardize his advantage.

'Perhaps because of this chivalrous and misguided belief, obviously shared by many of you out west, the exchange will go more smoothly and efficiently,' the Boss responded in his educated and southern aristocratic manner.

'What was that?' Mason responded gruffly, obviously not familiar with some of the words the Boss had just used in his complicated sentence.

With an exaggerated sigh, the Boss responded very slowly, 'Perhaps I should use smaller words. As I have stated before, if our opponents feel the same as you, then perhaps they will trade.'

'I ain't going to trade no woman!' Mason said. Mason was known for his hot temper as well as his speed with a gun. Few were as fast, and in reality, none in this group could compete. It was his confidence in his abilities that pushed Mason into this confrontation with the Boss.

'Anybody else feel as Mason?' the Boss said, exasperated with this useless confrontation.

There were a lot of downcast eyes as the Boss looked from face to face. 'I guess your opinion doesn't carry the support of your peers,' the Boss said as he extended his right arm and swung it in a wide arc, indicating the rest of the gang. As he swung his arm, a hideout gun, one of the brand new and very small .22 caliber Remington Vest Pocket pistols, slipped into his hand, and when he again faced Mason, he pulled the trigger. It happened so fast that Mason could only look on in shock as a perfectly round hole appeared in his shirt front, right where his heart was. The hole even smoked a bit from residual powder at so close a range – and soon turned to crimson. Mason took an involuntary step back as his body absorbed the impact of the small bullet, while he continued looking down at the growing bright red stain. The other members of the gang were just as shocked as Mason. They knew their Boss was tough and that he was also fast on the draw, but no one knew he carried a hideout gun. No one even suspected the Boss had a hideout except Oliver.

To ensure against his hideout gun only maiming Mason, the Boss then drew his left-hand gun and brought it level, just in case. After a second, he knew he wouldn't need it and holstered it again. Silence and disbelief continued as Mason slowly crumpled to the ground, dead before he landed with his shocked expression frozen on his face.

'Does anyone else wish to object to my new plan?' the Boss asked simply, the small caliber pistol still held in his hand. 'Ranger? You had concerns?' Ranger simply shook his head as he stared at his fallen comrade.

When no one objected, the Boss calmly stated that the crew could divide up Mason's belongings and he would put Mason's share back in the pot for distribution. 'Don't bother burying the body for when we leave here, we aren't coming back. If you want, you may drag him over behind the rocks out of the way.' Then as an afterthought the Boss said, 'Oh, and the ten dollar gold piece I lost to Mason in a bet over the fight, I want that back.'

There was an even greater and more awkward silence following the Boss's emotionless statement, but it was interrupted by Oliver, who was guarding Vivian, and who said, 'She's awake!'

# TEN

Vivian's mind slowly became aware again and tried to ascend back to consciousness. It was as if she were buried deep in snow and was trying desperately to climb out, but the snow held her fast and smelled and tasted terrible. Her every move was a struggle. Her head hurt and she was disoriented. She couldn't breathe, then realized she had a filthy bandanna stuffed in her mouth, and it was secured by another bandanna. The smell and taste of the filthy bandanna made her gag. Her hands were tied behind her and her feet were tied at the ankles. She knew it was still night and was aware of the flickering of a fire. She was lying on the ground in the midst of a group of attentive shadows. Suddenly a figure loomed over her. 'She's awake,' she heard the dark figure say. Soon there were other faces looking down at her, and she recognized none of them.

'Well, well,' the Boss said. 'Welcome to our reality.' Vivian struggled to sit up. She tried to push the gag from her mouth with her tongue, but couldn't. Her eyes went wide with fear as she struggled to breathe. But she knew that fear and panic wouldn't help her, so she relaxed and let her trained mind focus upon her surroundings. It was then that she heard a new and cultured voice, and saw a new, prominent face come into her view. She studied the face that was speaking. It was dark in shadow and was mottled from the flickering of the struggling fire, but it was an aristocratic, confident face. The voice had a southern accent, and the language suggested the man was obviously educated. 'Remove her gag,' the voice said.

Once the gag was removed and she could finally take an unflavored breath, it all came back to her – the stagecoach, the firefight, the attractive young man... She was surrounded by several attentive men as she struggled to roll over and finally sit up. It was obvious to her that she had been brought here against her will. Her head hurt, which implied that she had been knocked out. She looked from face to face: most had looks of concern, some had disassociated interest, and one even leered with intensity.

She obviously had a part to play here, so she calmed herself. 'What am I doing here?' Vivian demanded. 'Untie me!'

'Soon, very soon,' the Boss said.

'Where is my handbag?' Vivian asked.

'Just like a woman, she wants her handbag even in this situation,' the Boss said.

'I have her bag,' Oliver said. 'She had it around her arm when I took her,' he said, holding it up. Then passing the handbag to the Boss, the Boss hefted it and spread the drawstring closure.

'Look what we have here,' the Boss said as he extracted the small .32 revolver. 'Our little bee has a stinger, and what a stinger it is. I don't think I've ever seen such a ladylike pistol. Of course I can't imagine a true lady carrying or even needing such a weapon.'

Vivian looked at the Boss and said, 'That is my gun. It was given to me by my uncle. He wanted me to be safe.'

'No need for you to worry your pretty head over this weapon anymore. We will take care of you, Miss? Miss?'

'Vivian,' Vivian said, as she brought her tied hands up to her eyes. When she again lowered her hands her eyes were red and irritated and welling up with tears. 'You have me tied up and are scaring me. What are you going to do to me?'

'Now don't you worry, Miss Vivian,' the Boss said as he looked around the men to see if anyone else caught on to her deception. 'As I said, we'll take good care of you.'

'I want to go home,' she said as her watering eyes sparkled in the flickering light. Then hanging her head, letting her tears slide down her face into the dust, she said very timidly, 'Please don't hurt me.'

Feeling sorry for her, Ranger spoke up: 'Boss, she's hog tied. Can't we untie her? We'll watch her.'

'We don't know what other stingers this bee may possess,' the Boss said, knowing Vivian had purposefully irritated her eyes to produce her tears. 'You never know with women. She might be faking this whole thing.'

'I want my mother,' Vivian cried. 'I just want to go home.'

'Boss?'

'I'm sorry, Miss Vivian, but I can't afford that you somehow get away. And I applaud your performance. The tears were a nice touch. I have seen many female performances and I admit yours is most convincing, especially for men of limited experience,' the Boss said, looking at the gullible circle of attending sympathizers.

With considerable effort, Vivian kneeled up and started wiping her tear-stained face with her dirty hands, making and smearing mud on her cheeks and crying silently. She started snuffing her nose and pathetically asked for her handkerchief. The Boss looked in her bag and said, 'I am sorry, Miss Vivian, but there is no handkerchief here.'

'There has to be,' Vivian sobbed. 'It matches my dress and handbag.'

'Here, use mine,' the Boss finally said, withdrawing an embroidered white silk handkerchief from the inside pocket of his coat and handing it over to Ranger, who then brought it over and, kneeling in front of Vivian, extended it to her.

Snorting in disgust and definitely ignoring her sobs, the Boss shook his head and called for Casper to follow him. They walked over and the Boss began speaking quietly with Oliver, 'I need you and Casper to go and talk with the three men at the stagecoach. Tell them you will exchange Vivian for the map.'

'Map?' Oliver asked, shocked at the revelation.

'One of them will know what I am speaking about,' the Boss said. 'Tell them that if they want to see the girl alive again, they must give us the map. Set up a time for the exchange, and we'll all be there.'

'Alive?' Casper asked in shock, and louder than he had meant to – then quietly said, 'You're thinking you might kill the girl?'

At that point Vivian began to sob loudly back at the fire, and asked 'What are you going to do with me? Are you going to kill me?' Her question perked up the rest of the assembly.

'Now, Boss, we were going to threaten to kill her, but we'd never actually kill her,' Oliver said quietly. 'They'll know we ain't serious and…'

'You leave that to me,' the Boss said defiantly to the two men, who were looking from Vivian to the Boss and then back again. 'I suggest one of you stay back and guard the other. Come back with their answer.'

'You're not coming, Boss?' Casper asked, and then shot a look at Oliver.

'You don't need me,' the Boss replied. 'Just come back with the time of the exchange.'

'Okay, Boss. First light,' said Oliver as he looked over at Casper, who met his eyes. 'You up for this Casper, I mean with that serious wound you've been nursing?'

'I'm up for anything you can come up with,' said Casper. 'The wound bled some, but I've had worse.'

'Okay, let's grab a couple hour of shuteye and then we'll light out.'

The two men left the circle of concerned men, who sympathetically continued to stare at the tear-stained and muddied face – which in turn was carefully studying the men around her. The Boss looked on, unsympathetic and even somewhat amused.

# ELEVEN

The sun hadn't yet made its appearance but the eastern sky was already beginning to glow. Radiating fingers of light were forming up and were just now reaching upward to illuminate another cloudless day that was destined to be hot. Yes, it would be another scorcher and so Rory had been up and looking for their attackers' sign for a while now. Anything he could do before the sun started beating down upon him was worth it.

With the first light of day, Rory had gone over and over the tracks, determining locations, confirming the dead and counting the remaining enemy. The visual evidence made it obvious that Vivian had either been kidnapped or killed and her body taken. He found where she had been dragged and where her kidnappers had put her upon a horse. Rory believed she was still alive, and he would act upon that assumption until he had evidence to the contrary.

Rory wanted to act, but unfortunately the tracks left by the departing survivors led in all different directions so he could not determine their origin or destination, and where Vivian may have been taken. Obviously the group had divided and approached from different directions to avoid being tracked, and had left in the same fashion.

Rory was now just waiting for Lowe so that Lowe could stay with Foré while he went following the set of tracks left by the horse he believed was carrying Vivian. He was sure that the tracks would converge together at some point, and wanted to know where his enemy lurked and where Vivian might be held.

As Rory was making some notes in the tally book he carried in his breast pocket, Lowe walked up. 'I checked on Foré. He is doing okay. You might want to check out his wound again. I ain't had much experience taking care of wounds...' he paused for effect, and then continued, '... just giving them.'

Rory caught the humor, but was not in the mood for jokes. Vivian was gone and he felt responsible. 'I'll look in on him in a few minutes,' Rory finally responded.

'You should see him,' Lowe said with a chuckle. 'He stripped the guns from the man he killed and strapped them on hisself. Luckily the man he killed was as big as is. Right now he is inspecting his new weapons. I never thought Foré would man up, but he's trying.'

'He's got grit,' Rory said. 'He may not know what to do, but once he understands, he does it.'

'Yea, I see it,' Lowe said. 'He raised the alarm last night and even though he was shot he still managed to shoot his attacker. For a first-timer, that takes grit.'

'I agree. He'll do.'

'So what do you make of our attackers?' Lowe finally asked. 'And what are we going to do about Vivian?'

'I figure there were at least sixteen men in the raid,' Rory said looking off in an easterly direction. 'It seemed two held back over there and watched the others attack. I believe that after our armed response one of those two men somehow got in from behind and knocked out Vivian and then dragged her out,' Rory said. 'I don't believe they killed her, or at least there is no evidence of that. Whether kidnapping Vivian was their main objective or not, doesn't matter now. What matters now is that they have her!'

After a second Rory squatted on his haunches and then continued, 'Their attack was carefully planned, but they obviously underestimated our preparedness. I counted six dead. Of the ten that got away, I don't know how many were wounded. For them, losing over a third of their number makes for a very costly attack.'

'With those losses, they will either give up, or come at us with everything they got,' Lowe said. Then pointing to the area where Rory had said the leader had observed the attack he asked, 'What's your take on their leader?'

'Not sure,' Rory said, 'It depends on how ruthless he is. I found sign that he stood back and just watched the attack, like a general observing the battle. He seems very willing to let his men die for his cause. A frontal assault is pretty risky in any situation, so I figure he is either very confident, perhaps a bit over-confident, or he just doesn't care for his men. I also reckon that either he has a real tight leash on his men, or some of them, especially after tonight, might reconsider their loyalty. Men of this type may be scoundrels, but they usually have friendships within their group. I am sure someone lost a friend last night, and I'll bet that that someone is none too pleased.'

'Maybe they'll forget this whole thing?' Lowe asked hopefully.

'Not if they took Vivian,' Rory replied.

'Yea, that's true. So you think they took Vivian to trade?' Lowe asked

'I do.'

'The sun is nearly up,' Lowe said, looking around. 'I say we wait for them to come and make a trade.'

'If you are right, they'll probably want your map,' Rory said in reply.

Rory could see Lowe was struggling with his comment. He knew Lowe had taken money for the job and he wanted to see it through, but he now had a dilemma, for he had the only thing they both believed the attackers wanted. Rory could see the wheels turning in Lowe's mind, and was convinced that Lowe was a decent man according to his own standards. Lowe's standards might be a little on the low side, but he definitely had a code of conduct. Rory chuckled at his own pun.

'What if we attacked them?' Lowe asked.

The suggestion surprised Rory. 'Well, that would definitely be a tactic the enemy would not consider. The only problem would be with Vivian's safety. She might be shot in the chaos.'

'Maybe,' Lowe said grudgingly. 'If we attacked them, we'd better be sure and get at least four right off to even up the odds, or we might end up in a gunfight we may not win.'

'You, in a gunfight you might not win?' Rory asked teasingly.

'Not likely, until now,' Lowe said. 'I don't play the odds. No gambling here, not with my life or the lives of my team at risk.'

Well, that was it, Rory thought. Lowe was thinking of him and Foré as his team. And Lowe was now seriously considering going against superior odds to rescue Vivian. A rescue where they both might die. It was one thing to steal from a traitor, as Lowe had been labeled by the Union Secret Service; it was another to steal from a friend. Sounds crazy, but Rory couldn't help but think of Lowe as a friend – well, not so much a friend, but at least as an ally. That thought seemed even worse the more he thought of it.

Somehow Rory would have to find a way to save everyone, while not confronting Lowe directly. Perhaps he could steal the map without Lowe finding out. He dismissed that thought, as it would require an intimate knowledge of where the map was hidden, and he felt he would forever regret having betrayed Lowe. Maybe he should try honesty with Lowe? No, it would become a matter of honor leading to the confrontation Rory wished to avoid. No, there had to be another way.

'So what is so special about that map?' Rory asked.

After a long moment of hesitation, Lowe said, 'It is a map of a gold mine. I am supposed to deliver it to a Major General Hawkins of the Confederate army in California, who is trying to recruit men. Beyond that, I don't know, and I don't really care.' And with that Lowe casually slid up his left pants leg and pulled a small oilskin envelope from his boot. He opened it and handed a folded sheet to Rory. Rory took it and unfolded it. He quickly perused it, not wanting to seem overly interested. He looked at Lowe, looked back at the map, then again looked at Lowe. He then folded it up again and handed it back to Lowe, who put it back in the envelope and replaced it in his boot.

'You think it is a legitimate map?' Rory asked, watching Lowe's reaction to his question very carefully.

'I really don't care. I was paid to deliver it, but now I would gladly return the money if I could. None of this would have happened had I just not taken the job.'

'Can you get out of it, the job I mean?'

'Nope. I took money so I have to see this through. You're a man of your word, so you understand.'

Rory nodded his head. He was just about to go and see to Foré when he heard Lowe say, 'Hey, look what we have coming our way!'

Rory looked up to see two men on horseback casually riding up to their camp. They looked haggard, as if they hadn't had a lot of sleep. One had a bandage on his arm, and Rory wondered whether that was the man he had hit last night, but who had run off.

When they were about fifty yards away, the one with the bandage shucked his gun and stopped, while the other kept walking his horse toward Rory and Lowe. At about twenty-five yards Rory called out, 'That is far enough. What do you want?'

'Name's Oliver, and that ugly toad behind me is Casper,' the man said. 'You speak for the group?'

Rory walked over to Lowe who nodded his head. 'I reckon, but I want nothing to do with kidnappers of women,' Rory said.

'Now hold on there,' Oliver said raising his hands in what he obviously considered a calming, reassuring gesture. 'She ain't been harmed, nor will she if you give us what we want.'

'He said we don't deal with abusers of women,' Lowe said.

'I don't like this situation any better than you, but our Boss don't allow us to question. We do what he says, and he says he wants some map you got. He says if you give us the map, he'll give you back your lady friend.'

'You tell your Boss he's no better than a bloodsucking tick on the backside of a mule,' Lowe said.

'Well now, I may agree with you there, but he'd kill me for saying so, so I ain't saying. All I knows is he wants the map pretty bad, and we are here to tell you how it is.'

'If we don't deal, what is he going to do?' Rory asked.

'Now I am not right sure,' Oliver said rubbing his stubbly jaw, 'but I wouldn't put nothin' past him. I wouldn't have thought he'd kill one of his own, but he did. You hear the shot last night?' The question caused Rory and Lowe to look at each other, then back at Oliver. 'He done shot Mason down. He cheated because nobody was as fast as Mason, but the Boss killed him and didn't even blink an eye. If he done that, who knows what he'll do…' Oliver let the sentence hang there, open to any and all interpretations.

Harming a woman out west was taboo, but apparently this 'Boss' of theirs did not subscribe to this unwritten law. 'Does your Boss know that he could be hung for even suggesting harming a woman?' Rory asked.

'I don't think he knows that, as he's not from around here, but I don't think that would even matter. He's a hard-driven man. He knows what he wants, and he fully expects to get it.'

'You think he might hurt the lady?' asked Lowe incredulously.

'I hope not, but as I said, he doesn't care much about anyone or anything but what he wants.'

'How could you follow and be loyal to such a man,' Rory paused for emphasis, then finished his sentence, 'or rather an animal like that?'

'Well now, that is a question I have been asking myself since he killed Mason. I don't like it any better than you, but I reckon I have to do it because I need the pay. I have spent too much time on this not to get paid.'

'You'd even sell your soul?' Rory asked.

Rory could tell that last comment hurt, as Oliver involuntarily flinched at the question. There was definitely a conflict going on in Oliver's mind. Oliver turned and looked back at Casper. There was no love lost between these two men, but the look that passed between them seemed to suggest otherwise. These two didn't see eye to eye on anything, but for the first time it seemed they had found common ground... revulsion. It then occurred to Oliver that maybe the reason the Boss had sent them together was *because* there was no love lost between them, and that maybe he was counting on either one of them being willing to betray the other. Oliver seemed to consider this for a long time.

So far Casper hadn't said anything. He had looked on while Oliver had done the talking, but he had been listening intently. When Oliver looked back at him, Casper could tell by the look on Oliver's face that he loathed what he was doing.

Casper hated Oliver, but probably not as much as he hated what they were doing. Was the money worth this? They had different fathers, but they had been raised pretty much together and by the same mother. A mother who loved them and who had instilled in them at least a minimal set of standards. They definitely were not on the path their mother had hoped, and were now what she would have called 'bad men', but she had laid down the law with a moral line they wouldn't cross, at least Casper thought so.

As Casper looked at Oliver, all he could think of was how disappointed his mother would be with the two of them. He was willing to ride off and forget this whole business if he knew Oliver felt the same, but the problem was he couldn't be sure. In the current situation, he couldn't tell Oliver what he was thinking, and anyhow he wasn't sure how Oliver would respond.

It appeared to Casper that even though Oliver was as disgusted with this whole thing as much as he was, it still looked like Oliver was going to cross that moral line. In response to Oliver's look, Casper could only shrug his shoulders with a lift of his eyebrows and an inclination of his head, basically saying he was willing to take off and leave this sordid mess behind, but it was up to Oliver to make the decision. After the shrug he looked steadfastly at Oliver, seriously hoping Oliver would take his hint.

Whether Oliver saw or correctly interpreted Casper's indication was a moot point, as Oliver looked down and slowly shook his head. Turning back to Rory and Lowe and he said, 'Sorry, boys. I don't like this situation but I need the money.'

'Well then, consider your soul lost,' Rory said.

'I reckon,' Oliver said, his eyes cast down for just a moment. Oliver then looked up and like a defeated man with nothing to more to lose, said, 'You got to let me know your decision so I can return and tell the Boss.'

Rory had seen the wordless exchange between Oliver and Casper, and decided to test Oliver's resolve. 'Sorry to send you back to your Boss without our agreement, but as I said, we don't trade womenfolk.'

'Okay then,' Oliver said, and turned his horse and began to walk back to Casper.

When he reached Casper, Oliver just walked his horse right on past. So Oliver had made his decision, Casper thought, and turned his horse to follow his half-brother.

Watching them walk away, Rory shouted after them, 'Why don't you go tell your Boss that we don't deal with lackeys, and if he wants something from us he needs to ask us himself.' Rory saw that Oliver had paused to hear him out before nodding his head in acknowledgment and walking away, followed by Casper.

As they started to leave, Lowe shouted, 'And tell your Boss that if there is one hair out of place on the girl's head, I will hunt down and kill the lot of you!'

'That was not what I had expected,' said Rory as he and Lowe watched the two men ride slowly away.

'How's that?' Lowe asked as they watched the figures grow smaller and blurry in the heated mirage of the desert air.

'Did you see their faces? The disgust? Neither one of them wanted any part of this swapping idea,' Rory said to Lowe as they continued to watch the now retreating dots. 'I venture there is a power struggle or at least a moral struggle going on within their ranks.'

'Their Boss must be a hard man. Hard enough to take a white woman for barter and be willing to kill one of his own to maintain his power,' Lowe offered. 'I imagine that don't sit well with the group.'

'I agree,' Rory said. 'He is a hard man, and women don't mean anything to him except what he can obtain through them. Remember he's already tried to kill Vivian once before, in the stagecoach, and we are lucky we survived. I think he will kill anyone, friend or foe, to get what he wants.'

'You think he is going to come and try to deal?' Lowe
asked.

'Don't know. Up to now he has kept his distance. Either
he is afraid, or he just doesn't want to get his hands dirty,'
said Rory.

'Well, I for one would love to meet him face to face.
If he kills his own, he is one bad hombre. Did you hear
what Oliver said? Said he cheated in his killing of that
Mason? So he must have used some hideout gun. Any
man who done that is more than bad, he is evil and
Oliver was right,' Lowe said. 'I wouldn't put anything
past him.'

'It is his men who are the flip card here,' Rory mused
out loud, 'and that might be our opportunity. The West
breeds some pretty hard men, but even men of this shadow
still have rules of behavior. And maybe we might be able
to use that. I could tell those two don't want anything to
do with this swap. They probably didn't realize it, but they
let slip some very important information. I believe there
is serious dissention in their ranks. They've lost six men
and their Boss is willing to kill members of his own gang.
Yea, they are desperate enough to try anything.' After an
extended pause Rory then said, pointing to the receding
tracks, 'And best of all, we now have obvious tracks back to
their camp. Maybe it is time for us to pay them an unan-
nounced visit.'

'There now, you and I are finally seeing eye to eye,'
Lowe said. 'I suggested that last night, but you waved it off.
Is it an option now?'

'Definitely. If you can get a larger enemy to hesitate
long enough, you can steal the victory.'

'Nice quote. Who said it?'

'My father. A lot of what he says makes sense to me now. When this is over I think I need to go visit him and Ma. I need to make amends and leave on good terms.'

Lowe was silent for a minute, and Rory could tell he seemed to want to continue the conversation and perhaps even to share, but seemed hesitant to open himself up. Rory waited, letting his silence encourage Lowe. After a moment Lowe said, 'I wish I had the chance to do that with my father. Unfortunately both he and my mother died before I was full growed. Spent most of my childhood in an orphanage. When I'd had enough of that I struck out on my own. Must have been all of twelve year old.

'Not to pry but how'd your parents die?

'Boat accident.'

When Rory looked puzzled, Lowe continued, 'A small paddlewheel on the Mississippi. The captain was pushing it too hard and he overtaxed the boiler. It blew. I was ten, and from what I understand, I'm lucky to be alive. I was fished out of the water, but my father and mother didn't make it.'

'They've been running paddlewheels on the Mississippi near seventy-five years now,' Rory exclaimed. 'It seems to me that by now, traveling that way would be safe. Was it an experimental boiler design?'

'No. Just greed.'

Another clue to Lowe, Rory thought. He had lived a rough life. No wonder he was as hardened as he was. Losing parents at that age was especially rough, and then being shipped off to an orphanage. What amazed Rory was that somewhere along the way Lowe had picked up the idea of integrity and serious loyalty. Rory wondered when he had started slinging a gun.

'Let's fill in Foré with our plans and leave before it gets dark. We want to be able to observe their camp and make our plans,' Rory said.

'Sounds good to me! Just sitting here doing nothing drives me crazy,' Lowe said. 'I'm ready to take it to them.'

# TWELVE

It was late afternoon when Oliver and Casper neared their camp. It had been a long and silent walk back. The sun had beaten down on them, and like their horses with heads hanging, they plodded slowly. Neither of the two seemed talkative – not that they really cared to talk to each other anyway – but now there was a silent undercurrent further dividing them. They would be arriving with unwelcome news.

The gang was lounging around when the two showed up. There was no shade where they had made camp save a few creosote bushes and these were being used to maximum but little effect as the sun was high and beating down. Vivian was sitting on her rock under guard. Her legs and hands were still tied but she was watchful and alert. Only the Boss stood as his two emissaries slowly plodded into camp. The fact that none of the other men even bothered to get up was not lost on the Boss. This lack of enthusiasm was telling. It seemed to the Boss that he was losing his men's respect and they lacked the willingness to complete the job.

'Well?' the Boss asked quietly.

Casper nodded his head to Oliver, who stood with his hands on his hips and head angled down, but his eyes looked up to his Boss. 'They said no deals over a kidnapped woman.' He didn't say it loud for fear the others of the gang would hear, which he saw the Boss seemed to appreciate.

After pacing back and forth in agitation, the Boss stopped and leaning forward quietly said, 'They understood I will kill her if they don't give me the map?'

'I made that very clear, but they called your bluff. They ain't afraid of us, and they both look like salty men. So what are we going to do?' Oliver asked the Boss.

'We will go give them a visit with the woman in tow and we will see if seeing her will change their mind.'

'And if they call yer bluff again, what are you going to do? You know harming that woman might get you killed even by some of our own men.'

'You leave the men to me,' the Boss said as he turned to go and address the rest of his men.

'Men, we need to plan,' the Boss called out. When he had their attention he continued, 'Men, we need to force the issue or we don't get our money, so all of you gather around. All but you Oliver. You keep an eye on our prize.'

The men slowly got up, most beating the dust from their pants with their hats, and approached where the Boss stood. A circle was formed, and when the Boss felt he had everyone's undivided attention, he began, 'We gave an ultimatum to those at the stagecoach. They were not willing to deal. We offered the woman for the item of value.'

No sooner did those words leave the Boss' mouth when there was a murmured undercurrent amongst the men.

'Now men, I know how you feel and I totally agree with you. I never would have harmed this woman. I was hoping we could resolve this stand-off peacefully without further loss of life. The question we have to answer now is what are we going to do?' The Boss looked around at his men. 'As some of you have questioned my leadership, I am open to suggestions. What do you recommend?'

This was a first for some of the men. They were used to being the muscle behind planned events; they had never actually planned them. The men looked around at each other. Some shrugged their shoulders, other inclined their heads, but no one spoke. After a few awkward seconds the Boss said, 'You all signed up knowing that to be paid we needed to obtain something of value. We have not been successful and if we don't do something, all is for naught. Our friends will have died for nothing.'

The Boss knew that last comment might inspire some loyalty, and possibly foster a need for vengeance of sorts amongst the men. He continued, 'Should we escort the woman back? Do you want to attack again? What do you suggest we do?'

The men continued to stand silent. Finally Casper said, 'We know that we would never harm this woman, but they don't know that. I think that if we all went to their camp with the woman, we might still make a trade.'

'Yea,' said Ranger. 'They don't know we won't hurt her, and if they see her, maybe they will trade.'

'Maybe she will beg for her life?' said Roscoe hopefully.

'And if they call our bluff?' the Boss said.

'Why don't we approach with only half of us,' Casper said. 'The rest might try circling around and shoot them when they show themselves.'

'Yea,' said Ranger. 'I like that!'

What then followed was a lot of talking, sharing ideas and noise. After a while the Boss finally raised his hand, calling for attention. 'Makes sense to me,' the Boss said, seeing that a consensus was building. 'So our plan is that we will return tomorrow morning to trade the girl for the prize. Roscoe, Casper and Curtis will circle around and get on top of the ridge behind them to take them from behind. We will try to trade, but if that fails I will raise my hat and that will be the signal for everyone to open fire.

So this is our plan?'

'One thing, Boss,' Ranger said. 'What are we trading the girl for?'

'I didn't share that with you before,' the Boss said, 'but now that we are all partners you need to know that we will be securing something so valuable that you will live as kings when we are done. Each of you is looking at $5,000 at least.' This news was met with enthusiastic approval, so the Boss again asked, 'Are we all in agreement?'

Oliver had been listening in. He well knew what the prize was, as did Casper. Oliver didn't know whether the Boss had already secured a buyer for the map, but he was surprised at the Boss's suggestion that each man's take would be in the range of $5,000. Suggesting that it would be $5,000 to each of the men, and being so open and cooperative about his plans, was not like the Boss at all. That being the case, he decided he would remain very wary.

Another observer was also listening in. Vivian was aware of the shifting dynamics of the group while she was considering her own options. Her bonds were a joke and she could have cut them and freed herself at any time, but she was a careful planner herself and would only take action when she knew it would yield fruit. She had been watching all day, and she knew men. She did not believe the Boss was being truthful. He was planning something, something which included her. What it was she had no clue, but men like the Boss did not suddenly turn democratic and give up control. She would bide her time and act when appropriate.

At the Boss's question, the men looked around at each other as if to test the visual waters. A couple began speaking quietly to the men next to them. At first they all were thoughtful, but then some began to nod. When it appeared there was a consensus the Boss again asked, 'Are we all in agreement?'

All the men each either nodded or said 'Yes'.

When they had all confirmed their support of the plan, Casper spoke up: 'Since we are all now helping in the planning, I think we should all have equal shares… including you,' he said, pointing to the Boss.

Silence followed. All the men looked at the Boss, wondering what he would do. Casper was known for his skill with a firearm, and was equal or better than all, including the Boss, at least in a stand-up fight. Even Oliver was taken aback by Casper's boldness. Mason's body was still warm and here was Casper challenging the Boss again.

You could have heard a snake slithering in the sand, the camp was so quiet. Everyone looked back and forth between the two men. Casper was standing directly in front of the Boss with legs spread and with his hands casually next to his gun butts. The Boss regarded him coolly. How he wanted to cut this man down, but he knew he might not be able to beat Casper in a fair fight, and he had already played his ace in the hole with his hide-out gun. He could see in Casper's eyes that if he made any move to get to his hideout, Casper would shoot. The tension lasted only a few seconds when the Boss finally nodded his head and said, 'All right. That is fair. We will all get an equal share, but I must be paid back for the supplies I purchased before we equally divide the rest.' This sense of fair play seemed to appease even the most skeptical of the group, and they all gathered closer when the Boss continued, 'Okay, let's go over the plan one more time.'

The men looked on as the Boss began drawing a diagram in the sand of the camp they would be approaching tomorrow and where the attempted exchange would take place. Everyone shared in recreating the camp as they remembered it, each giving suggestions on the best approaches, any obstacles, fields of view, and the best vantage points. The suggestions came fast and plentiful as everyone wanted success, more so now because now they had a vested interest in the outcome.

The Boss seemed very pleased with the direction the meeting had taken. He appeared very agreeable, and presented a sincere and accommodating demeanor. The discussion and planning lasted the rest of the afternoon and into the evening. How sincere he was didn't seem to weigh on anyone except Oliver, who was still guarding Vivian and hadn't participated in the discussion.

Oliver looked on, wondering whether the others knew the caliber of man they were dealing with. The Boss was one of the most ruthless men Oliver had ever known, and that was saying a lot. Knowing this, Oliver questioned just about anything the Boss said and did, but he always kept his questions to himself. He wasn't about to disagree with the Boss, because he had seen what happened to any who disagreed with him.

Oliver knew how the Boss responded to threats. The Boss was totally unpredictable. He could be explosive and lash out, or he would just let the disagreement fester before taking deadly action. Thoughts regarding the Boss were best kept to oneself, something Oliver knew from experience. He just had to look at Mason's corpse behind the rocks to confirm this. Oliver had long suspected the Boss possessed a hideout gun, and had assumed he was willing to use it. Mason was probably not the first to be killed with that gun, nor would he be the last. Killing a member of your own team with a hideout gun, if that wasn't an indication of the treachery of the man, nothing was.

As Oliver watched the goings on, he doubted the Boss was really as accommodating as he seemed to be. To Oliver it seemed that this was all just an act to get the gang to come together again. The Boss was still just using them, and much to Oliver's dismay it appeared that the men, including Casper, had taken the bait, hook, line and sinker. Oliver wondered what Casper thought of all this. Though they were always fighting each other, Oliver thought he knew Casper well enough to believe he wouldn't be so easily duped by the Boss. But then again, maybe Oliver was giving his half-brother too much credit.

Perhaps Oliver should warn Casper about the Boss. Even though Casper was his enemy, Oliver still considered him blood. Thin blood perhaps, but still blood, nevertheless. Oliver continued to watch the proceedings, but as always, Oliver kept all his thoughts to himself. He had to look out for himself, and watch and see just how accommodating the Boss really would be.

# THIRTEEN

Mounting the horses they had chosen, Rory and Lowe left a little before twilight to ensure there would be sufficient light to follow the tracks left by Oliver and Casper. Knowing they would be riding bareback they had picked the most responsive of the three remaining horses, but being used to pulling a stagecoach, the horses demonstrated their displeasure by stamping, snorting and trying to dislodge their riders. But after a bit of irritation the horses accepted their mounts and the pair finally trotted off, following the tracks.

From the sound of the gunshot they had heard the night before, the pair believed the enemy camp was not more than five miles away. In time they were gratified to see the light of a small camp fire, and they headed in that direction.

They tethered their horses about two hundred yards away from the camp on some grass amidst some pinion pine and juniper, and then carefully approached the camp on foot. When they were within a hundred yards they could see their enemy hadn't even bothered to set up a sentry, so they closed the distance to within fifty yards.

Rory, ever prepared, produced a small and powerful telescope: after observing the camp he handed it over to the surprised Lowe. Lowe took the telescope, and turning it over in his hands, quietly expressed his admiration. 'I never knew a man to be so prepared. What else you got tucked away?'

Rory just nodded and quietly chuckled, 'Give a look so we can plan.'

Lowe put the telescope to his eye and carefully scanned the layout, going from right to left then left to right, carefully committing the layout to memory. Once he seemed satisfied with his overview, he said, 'They've got Vivian over on the left and she doesn't seem to be hurt. She's alert, and doesn't seem to be scared to me,' Lowe whispered in amazement. 'In fact, she seems relaxed, almost as if she is just inconvenienced, not kidnapped and threatened. She's just sitting on a rock out in the open. Her legs are tied at the ankles and her hands at the wrists. That guy, Oliver, seems to be guarding her.' Lowe looked again through the eyepiece and was silent for a while, then grunted and handed the telescope back to Rory. 'Check out the dandy on the far left, the one with the dress coat and tie, if you can believe it!'

Rory took back the telescope and after a brief look snorted and said, 'Dandy is right. That may be the Boss Oliver spoke of. We've been here for a full day and night now, and he looks like he's dressed for church. Look at his boots. No spurs, and though dusty, I can see the quality from here and they are definitely not Western boots. Yea, he is quite the dandy, but he is also well heeled.'

'Yea,' said Lowe. 'It looks like he favors a brace of Colts.'

'You think he is the Boss?' Rory asked.

'That's my bet. You know his coat is cut in the longer southern style. I wonder if he ain't a southern gentleman,' Lowe said with a sarcastic edge to his whisper.

'Southern maybe, gentleman, no,' Rory quietly said. 'Gentlemen do not ransom women and threaten them with death, or use a hideout gun on their own men. The question is, why is he tied up with this riff raff? And how does he know about your map?'

'All good questions,' Lowe said. 'Perhaps when he is breathing his last, he might get a chance to answer 'em.'

The two men returned to their horses and prepared for a brief night's sleep. They would only have a few hours, and needed to be up and ready long before their enemy was. The night was warm so no blankets were necessary. They even left their horses saddled just in case. Tomorrow this would all be over, and either Rory and Lowe would be successful in bringing Vivian back with them, or one or even both of them would die.

While they were lying in the sand and waiting either for sleep to come or for the night to end, Rory said, 'We counted nine men and the Boss.' After a pause he then added, 'Are you really as good with those hogs of yours as you say?'

'What do you think?' Lowe asked.

'I'm not really sure. I've known only a few gunmen, and every one of them thought they were the fastest.'

'Well, you saw me taking off the head of that rattler.'

'Yea. That was a good shot, but that snake wasn't shooting back,' Rory said.

Lowe chuckled at Rory's comment, then said, 'So what makes you think I'm a gunman?'

'I've only seen guns doctored like yours once before, and they belonged to a dead man who thought he was a gunman. Don't get me wrong,' Rory continued, 'he was fast, but not fast enough. It seems his custom guns didn't do him much good.'

'Well, I think you could say I'm a gunman and my custom guns definitely work.' Lowe paused, then said with a tinge of sadness in his voice, 'I've done my share of killing, but I don't look for fights. When you get a name for being fast, there's always someone who wants to test you.'

'And not many gunmen die of old age,' mused Rory.

'True enough – but now,' Lowe brightened, 'I'm in the security business – you know, the map thing.' Then turning on his side to watch Rory he asked, 'Did you know the name of the dead gunman you mentioned, the one with the doctored guns?'

'His name was Samuel Frost,' Rory said. 'He was called the Snowman, and he had a reputation of being a cold killer, which explains how he got the name.'

'When and where was he killed?' Lowe asked.

Sensing a strong interest flavoring Lowe's questions, Rory turned to face Lowe and said, 'It was in Independence, Missouri, about a year after the war broke out. He got into a confrontation with some Federal lawman. Did you know him?'

'Yea. He was an acquaintance is all, but he knew shooting irons. If fact it was Frost that doctored my six-guns, and he was going to set me up with what you got, rifle and pistol both shooting the metal .44 cartridge. I was wondering whether he set up your guns, but I saw that your rifle didn't have his stamp. He always stamped his work on the underside of the action.'

Rory let Lowe's comment hang a while, knowing what was coming next. It wasn't long before Lowe asked the question Rory was expecting: 'You know, I'm surprised he was killed. He was pretty fast. Know who fetched him?'

'I know it was just some sort of Federal law man,' Rory said, without elaboration. 'I was in Independence at the time and saw the aftermath. That's when I had a chance to inspect his guns. I can see how removing the front sight would ensure the gun draws faster out of the holster, but locking and then removing the trigger? I assume you have your triggers locked the same?'

'Let's just say I don't have to worry none about pulling a trigger,' Lowe said. 'Sad about Frost. He was an excellent gunsmith, and wasn't just good at making and fixing guns, he could shoot them as well. The man that took him had to very good.'

'How would you rate yourself against Frost?' Rory asked.

'No comparison. Frost was good, but I'm the best.'

'Well then, I'm glad you're on my side.'

'You want to see just how good I am, just wait till tomorrow,' Lowe said. 'You won't have to even shoot that fancy rifle of yours, as I expect I'll fetch all nine within a minute, maybe minute and a half. The only one I'm worried about is the Boss.'

'Well, unless you're shooting nine shooters, you're going to have to reload,' Rory said with a sarcastic edge.

'I'll fetch 'em all,' Lowe said confidently, ignoring the jibe. 'But do me a favor and be sure and take out the Boss if you can. There's something not right about him.'

Shortly after that last comment, Rory heard Lowe's slow, even breathing and knew he had fallen asleep. Rory doubted he could sleep, for whenever he knew he would be involved in a shooting, he would spend a sleepless night. Whether it was the fear of getting shot or killed, or the idea that he would be killing others, never sat quite well with him, and it would always drive sleep from his mind. Even if the men he was sent against deserved killing, it brought questions of the heart when he snuffed out someone's life. Perhaps it was his religious upbringing. His father wasn't interested in organized religion, but his mother was a staunch Presbyterian. He had gone many times with his mother to church, but it never seemed to stick. Things didn't add up the older he got, so in time he followed after his pa and focused on work.

So here he was again, about to engage in a life and death struggle where men would die. Even he might die. He had been the means of causing death several times, but it still caught something deep inside him. One minute a man is alive, he is a reasoning being, and the next he was useless meat. He felt the same when he butchered livestock, but at least their meat gave life. Here it would just be a waste. He remembered every one of those whose life he had ended. Every face and every event in minute detail. He even remembered the Snowman.

Their plan was simple. Just as the men were getting up for the day, they would strike. Rory would stay back and use his rifle while Lowe would wade into the camp with his six shooters. They believed that this element of surprise within the camp would allow them to easily eliminate most, if not all of the men. Lowe was particularly confident.

The night passed slowly, and Rory wondered whether he actually got any shuteye at all. He could hear Lowe's steady and deep breathing with an occasional sniff. Going to sleep so easily, Rory thought Lowe was definitely a cool customer.

Unbidden, both Rory and Lowe seemed to rise at the same time. It was just after four in the morning, and there was still no hint of day.

After sharing some pemmican and cheese they both checked their guns one last time. 'You sure you have enough ammunition for those hogs of yours?' Rory asked, just to make conversation.

'No question,' Lowe replied. 'I also brought two extra cylinders. So with twenty-four shots, that's almost three shots per man. More than enough – and that's assuming you don't catch a couple yourself with your fancy rifle.'

'So, when do you want to start the show?'

'When you hear the first shot, you open up,' Lowe said. 'It'll be a mad house, with everyone scrambling for cover. I will take everyone I can see, but watch my back. Okay?'

'I'll do my best. Are you confident?'

'Oh yes I am,' Lowe said with such assurance that Rory was a little taken back. 'I haven't met a man I couldn't kill,' he said with a matter-of-fact tone.

As the two men carefully walked back to the place they had used to observe the enemy camp Rory again considered Lowe's confidence – or rather, what he considered to be over-confidence. He accepted most of Lowe's statement as simple bravado. Of course Lowe hadn't met a man he couldn't kill, because if he had he would have been killed himself. This was the hitch in the thinking of all gunslingers. They thought they were the best... until they weren't.

He looked at Lowe, still expecting to see some signs of fear, but Lowe seemed totally calm and collected as he purposefully walked towards the camp. He acted as if this was just another day of chores. Even Rory felt a little skittish about the assault, and he wasn't the one going into the lion's den. Rory realized that Lowe might in fact be the coolest, most deadly man he had ever met, and he realized that maybe Lowe's statement might not be just bravado after all. Lowe really seemed that confident, and he appeared totally unfazed about what he was going to do.

Thinking back, Rory remembered that, after assessing the situation through the telescope, it was Lowe who had suggested that he show up in the camp by himself and throw down the attack. It was also his suggestion that Rory stay back and use his rifle to pick off those who found shelter from Lowe's assault, and ensure no one could shoot him from a blind spot. True, Lowe seemed to Rory to be the epitome of confidence, but no one could be that confident. But the more he thought of it, the more Rory concluded that either Lowe was hiding his apprehension perfectly, or he really *was* that confident. And if he *was* that confident, then heaven help those men tomorrow.

Lowe and Rory arrived at their designated place in plenty of time. There was still no sentry or sign of activity coming from the camp. The fire was down to coals. The sun hadn't shown itself yet, but the far sky was just beginning to glow yellow on the horizon, and Rory figured there was maybe thirty to forty minutes before the sun peeked over.

After taking a few minutes to relax, Lowe simply said, 'I guess it's time,' as he stood up. He interlocked his fingers, and raising his arms over his head, stretched and arched his back. He carefully retrieved a pair of very thin black leather gloves from his pocket, and slipped them on. He spread his hands several times ensuring the gloves were smooth and tight, each time causing the leather to stretch and creak to conformity. He slipped the thongs off the hammers of his guns, then rested his hands on his gun butts and jostled his guns to ensure they were loose and the holsters were positioned correctly. He then checked the two extra cylinders, which were carefully inserted in their special loops on his custom-made gun belt. He then took the guns out, one after the other, and blew out the actions, slowly spinning the cylinders, and inspected the rounds. He then replaced them back in their holsters and drew them both very slowly, and then again, this time faster. Rory concluded that this was Lowe's pre-war ritual. After several warm-up draws, both fast and slow, Lowe nodded. 'I'm ready.'

'Okay,' Rory said. 'I got your back.'

Lowe looked at the enemy camp for a few moments then quietly said, 'Be sure you watch out for that Dandy.' And without taking his eyes off the camp to even look at Rory, he carefully started walking toward the camp and his enemies.

Rory watched as Lowe approached the camp, quietly and efficiently. He didn't draw either gun; he just walked right toward the camp, his boots making no sound other than the muffled scuff of shifting sand. He skirted a few bushes and stepped over something, but kept pretty much a straight line.

Rory had inspected his rifle the night before, and again during Lowe's ritual, ensuring it was fully loaded. He then got to one knee and quietly jacked a shell into the chamber. He didn't know if and when Lowe would be discovered, but he wanted to be ready. He didn't bring the rifle up yet, as he needed to see where the danger to Lowe would come from, and where to place his shots.

# FOURTEEN

It took Lowe no more than a minute to enter the camp. He faced the remains of last night's fire, now down to coals, and assessed the sleeping men, one by one. A couple were snoring, one loudly. The dandy, or the man they had concluded was the Boss, was on the far right, as was Vivian. She was lying in the dirt, either asleep or feigning sleep, the man supposedly guarding her likewise. As Lowe watched her, she shifted slightly and Lowe believed that not only was she awake, but she was watching him. It was still too dark to actually see her eyes, but something in the way she shifted her weight led Lowe to believe she was awake and alert, as if curious to see what was going to happen.

For a good minute Lowe simply stood there assessing the camp. His head slowly shifted from left to right, his hands spreading and then balling into fists several times, his leather gloves creaking quietly, as he took everything in. Rory watched in amazement as Lowe just stood there with his guns in their holsters apparently evaluating and listening to the sleeping men. It was like Lowe was waiting for someone to discover his presence. A final offer of fair play, or just another example of his bravado?

After a long, agonizing minute, one of the men grunted, then mechanically sat up, rubbed his eyes, shook out his boots and slipped them on. He then stood up and stamped his feet deep into his boots before picking up and belting on his guns. The groggy man ran his fingers through his greasy, shaggy hair before picking up and jamming his hat on his head. He then slowly wound his way around his compatriots to the glowing coals from last night's fire. Rory guessed he was going to get coffee on.

The man began to look around as if to locate something when Lowe finally spoke. 'You just going to stand there?'

The man jerked around at the sound of Lowe's voice, and drew his gun as he did. He may have been considered fast by some, but he wasn't even close to matching Lowe. Lowe's guns were holstered when he spoke but when the man turned and palmed his gun, Lowe drew and shot from both his guns, the reports almost as if there was only one shot. The bullets took the man in the chest and sent him backwards into the coals of the night fire. The explosion of the guns and the screams of the dying man withering in the fire instantly brought the camp to life. Men scrambled to get their guns into action as Lowe calmly shot another man who was just bringing his gun level.

Rory watched as Lowe methodically took out those two men, and then he realized that Lowe wasn't just shooting men, he was shooting only those who were either shooting or about to shoot at him. After killing his first man Rory saw that Lowe reholstered his guns and waited for the next challenger. The second man got off a wild shot, but went down the same way as the first. Lowe turned to the new threat and drew, his guns blossoming flame, and the man went down. Once the man was down and slowly withering in the sand, Lowe again reholstered his guns.

Men began running everywhere, some shouting out questions and others giving commands, and a few throwing hasty shots into the air. Lowe calmly turned to his left as he saw a man kneeling with gun drawn about to shoot. After a blur of motion the man was suddenly thrown back by the bloody impact of Lowe's speed and accuracy. While this was going on, another man on Lowe's right rolled on the ground and brought his six-gun to bear, shooting wildly as fast as he could cock and pull the trigger. Rory sighted down his rifle and squeezed off a shot. The man's hand suddenly erupted. The gun was forcibly thrown to the left, taking with it several fingers and possibly a thumb. Rory jacked in another shell and fired again, ensuring the man was down and would stay that way.

After jacking another round into the chamber Rory was able to assess the camp again, but in the mêlée he had lost track of the Boss and Vivian. Both of them were gone, as was Vivian's guard. Rory swore under his breath.

The shouts in the camp became fewer as Lowe reduced the numbers. One man had taken refuge behind one of his dead comrades and after his first wild shot was bringing his gun more level. Lowe didn't have much of a target, as the man was hiding behind the body of his fellow, but Lowe drew and shot what he could see and the man took it between the eyes.

Lowe then killed another man who was courageously but foolishly charging with gun drawn and firing as he charged. The man's gun blossomed and Lowe was hit, causing him to drop his left-hand gun. Lowe didn't even flinch as he accepted the wound and the loss of the gun before drilling the man with his right gun twice. The first bullet stopped the man in his tracks, and the second toppled him backwards where he convulsively kicked at the dirt before breathing his last. Lowe holstered his now empty right hand gun and with his right hand picked up the gun he had dropped. He had efficiently killed five men and was now carefully looking around for his next victim. He had one bullet left and with his injury he would be unable to reload the nearly empty gun.

Rory was in a panic. He needed to find where the Boss and Vivian had gone, but before he could, another man, kneeling behind a bush and out of Lowe's field of vision, required Rory's attention. He couldn't see the man clearly, but it was only a bush so Rory shot mid center where he believed the man's chest would be. He was gratified to see the man fall back, his arms flung out, sending his gun flying. Lowe saw Rory's last shot and rushed over to ensure the man was dead. He was. Rory's bullet had hit dead center, with 'dead' being the key word. And with that last shot, the violent eruption stopped.

Both Rory and Lowe waited a few seconds, each carefully scanning the area. Rory thought he had heard the sound of horses during the mêlée but his focus had been in keeping Lowe alive. After a few seconds of quiet, Rory ran toward the camp to inspect the carnage. Lowe had now seated himself on the rock where Vivian had previously sat and was trying to replace the spent cartridges in both his guns. His wound was dripping blood and his hands were smearing it on his guns.

Rory had to step over two of Lowe's victims to get to him. He noticed both men were lying on their backs quite dead. Since now Rory knew Lowe usually shot twice when he shot, he knew Lowe was not just bragging about his being good – he was. Rory couldn't even tell whether those men had been shot more than once as the wounds seemed so close together. Rory had never seen such a display. It had appeared to Rory that Lowe had taken this whole event as an exercise and a personal challenge, which is why Lowe had re-holstered his guns after each killing. He had killed all these men on the draw except the last man who had charged him. Lowe hadn't time to re-holster but had turned slightly, and drilled the man. So last night Lowe had indeed been bragging, but with authority, and now Rory had confirmed it for himself, and with bloody confidence. Lowe was indeed as fast on the draw as he claimed, and was deadly, deadly accurate. Maybe he *was* the best.

Rory quickly went around to the other men to ensure they were all dead. They were. Seven men in probably a minute, just about as Lowe had predicted, though of course Rory could claim two of those. Looking at the carnage Rory believed that had the other three men remained behind, they would be just as dead as these unfortunate few scattered around the camp.

Death had come quickly and efficiently. Seven men were dead, but two were missing as well as the Boss. What concerned Rory was that Vivian was also missing, and he assumed those who had escaped had taken her with them. He knew he had to track them down and try to free Vivian, but he realized that because Vivian had been taken, she was obviously too important to kill. She would be safe, at least for the time being. Rory knew Lowe had been hit and Lowe needed his assistance for now, but once Rory was confident Lowe was okay, he would focus on Vivian.

\*\*\*\*

As soon as the firing began, the Boss awoke, and without getting up and attracting attention, he quickly scanned the situation. He saw Lowe calmly eliminating his men. He watched for just a second, hoping someone would take him out, but he quickly realized none of his men was up to the challenge. Perhaps Mason would have been capable, but he was unfortunately dead. The Boss considered trying to shoot Lowe himself, but when he saw Lowe had deadly back-up, he decided escaping was his best course of action. Keeping low, he crawled over to Vivian, and drawing his gun, put it to her head at the same time as he covered her mouth with his left hand. She nodded in understanding so he quickly took his hand off her mouth, picked up the gag that had been discarded in the dirt, and put it back in her mouth and secured it with a bandanna. He then began dragging her out of the commotion and toward the horses.

The Boss had set his blankets on the edge of the camp and far away from the others, as it did not seem proper that a gentleman should be sleeping in the company of his inferiors. As a result of this foresight he didn't have to crawl far to get Vivian out of the camp and away from the gunfire. When he was far enough away he pulled Vivian up, and slicing the rope on her feet, threw her on the closest horse. Keeping the horse's reins in his hand he quickly untied his own horse and then Vivian's from the common tether line. He was about to climb into his saddle when Casper, crawling around a bush to flank the shooter, looked over toward the horses and saw the escape in progress.

Kneeling up Casper said, 'Where you going, Boss?' Then as he realized the Boss was leaving with his prize he sarcastically said, 'Taking off with your prize? Don't you think the boys could use your help about now?'

Without any hesitation the Boss turned, and in so doing palmed his hideout gun and shot Casper in the chest. The man crumpled, and the sound of the shot simply died away amidst the cacophony of gun fire near them. Then mounting up and leading Vivian's horse, the two rode off into the growing light of morning, leaving the field of battle, just as he had done at the Battle of Port Royal. The Boss, Gerald Remington Harrison III, once again considered his men expendable – but this time they were not just expendable, they were also the fodder in allowing his escape.

Like Casper, Oliver, too, had scrambled out of his blankets, and keeping low, decided to flank the shooter. Just like his half-brother, he headed around back and near the horses. As he approached the horses he heard the sound of running hooves in the background of gunfire. As he got closer he noticed two horses were missing and a man was lying nearby. He recognized the clothes, and hurried over to his public nemeses, Casper, his belligerent half-brother. He knew he needed to flank the shooter but he still took the time to roll the body over and saw that Casper was still breathing, if you could call it that. From the blood and sucking sound coming from a chest wound and the red froth from his mouth, Oliver knew Casper had been shot in the lungs and that he was probably breathing his last. Casper's eyes were open, registering pain and fear as they locked on to his hated half-brother.

'The Boss,' Casper quietly bubbled. 'Hideout gun.'

'Why'd he shoot you?' Oliver asked incredulously, feeling guilty he hadn't warned Casper the type of man the Boss was.

140

'Coward. He took… woman.'

That last was said so quietly that Oliver had to put his ear next to Casper's frothing mouth to hear the dying man's whispers. Casper tried to say more, but nothing came out except the final hiss of his punctured lungs expelling their last breath.

With the sound of lessening gunfire, Oliver made his decision. He quickly ran to the horses, untied his personal mount and headed out in the direction taken by the Boss and Vivian. The Boss had a lot to answer for, but killing Casper was the last straw. Though there was no love lost between Oliver and Casper, still they were blood family, and nobody was allowed to kill his family except him. And nobody, including his half-brother, deserved to die at the hands of a traitor using a cheat gun.

**\*\*\*\***

The battle was over, and after confirming the dead, Rory turned his attention back to Lowe. Lowe's wound was not life threatening though he had bled a lot and it would leave a nasty scar. The bullet had struck in the upper left side of his chest, just below the armpit. It had broken the skin and glided along a rib for an inch before exiting, leaving an ugly wound. In exiting the bullet had sliced the flesh down to the ribcage, but the rib was sound as Rory was able to actually see the exposed rib. The wound was ragged and mean, but it would heal – it would take time and be very painful for a while, but it would heal. Of course, Lowe would be down to using only one gun, but somehow Rory didn't really think that would make a difference in Lowe's death-dealing potential.

Rory realized he needed to cauterize the entry wound and stitch the exit wound closed. He had no needle to stitch the exit wound, but he could cauterize the entry wound and bind the exit wound tightly until he could properly stitch it up. After outlining what he was going to do, over Lowe's protests Rory went to heat up his knife for the first part of his administrations. He had to drag a roasting body off the coals to heat his knife, but once allowed oxygen the coals glowed right up and Rory was able to heat his knife easily.

While Rory was treating the wound, Lowe, between gasps of pain, inquired after the missing men and Vivian: 'I didn't see the Boss during the fight. He escape?'

Rory could only nod his head. He knew he had done what was necessary to save Lowe, but still he had let those men slip out and they had taken Vivian. 'I'm afraid so,' was all Rory could muster through his self-incrimination.

'Well, you watched my back,' Lowe said. 'I saw the two you fetched. They would have got me for sure.'

Rory appreciated Lowe's understanding, but still felt he had somehow failed. 'Well, I have to hand it to you Lowe. You are as good as you say, maybe even the best.'

Lowe just grunted. 'These were bad men, but not gunfighters. I knew they didn't stand a chance.'

'During all the excitement, did you hear horses?' Rory asked. 'I went over and I found a man by the horses, a dead man. He was the one who came to deal for Vivian yesterday, and was at the back covering his partner. I didn't shoot him and he was out of your sight, so I think those who were running away had a difference of opinion. To make things even more confusing, I found another body behind the rocks over there,' Rory said, pointing to the left side of the camp, 'but that man has been dead for at least a day.'

'We didn't know about the day-old dead one, so with the one you just found that means there are only two of them with Vivian now,' Lowe said.

'That's what I figure,' Rory said.

'Now that I recall, I think I also heard horses, but I was too busy to worry about it,' Lowe admitted as he watched Rory bring the glowing knife to the entry wound.

'Now just hold still,' Rory said as he placed the knife.

'I think you're enjoying this,' Lowe said through clenched teeth amid the smoke and smell of searing flesh.

'Maybe so,' Rory said, nodding his head as he inspected the now scorched bullet hole. 'I still need to stitch up the exit wound but I don't have a needle here. I have one at our camp, but I think we have to follow those three before they get too far away.'

'Just get me to a horse,' Lowe said indignantly.

'You lost a sight of blood as the bullet laid open a flap of muscle,' Rory said. 'Now hold still so I can wrap this rope around you. We need to bind up this wound and limit the movement of your left arm or you will start bleeding again. I wish I could stitch you up, but as I said, I've no needle and we have to get going.'

'Then tie this rope off and let's vamoose,' Lowe said.

Rory paused in his administrations, and said, 'You will be limited to just your right arm.'

'I'm good with that,' Lowe insisted through clenched teeth as Rory tightened the wrapping around his torso.

'You good with only one hog?' Rory asked.

'After what you saw, what do you think?' Lowe asked. 'So where do you think they went?' he said, his voice reflected the pain he was experiencing as Rory swung another loop, binding Lowe's left arm to his side and across his chest.

'My guess is the Boss is still trying to get what he came after, and he thinks the map is back at the stagecoach.'

'Foré is there,' Lowe said, with apprehension in his voice.

'I know, and he may end up paying the price of my failure,' Rory admitted.

'Nope, I think Foré will do fine,' Lowe said, trying to sound confident but instead sounding rather unsure, 'but I do think we should hurry up and maybe help him some.'

'Well, you are cinched up tight now, so if you are done jawing, we can go,' Rory said.

'Just help me into a saddle,' Lowe stated, the flavor and intensity of his remark punctuated by his pain, impatience and frustration at his weakness.

Instead of retrieving their horses, Rory took two of the dead men's horses and led them back to where Lowe was sitting. Grabbing Lowe, Rory helped the now one-handed gunman up into the saddle. Then quickly looking around at the carnage, he said, 'We'll come back and clean up this mess later.'

'Nope,' Lowe said in disgust. 'We'll come back for the horses is all, but as for the men, let 'em lie. The vultures are too good for them.' Then with heels to his mount, he took off in the direction of the disabled stagecoach and Foré, with Rory hurrying to catch up.

# FIFTEEN

The Boss was indeed heading to the stagecoach as Rory has predicted, though he was taking a more circuitous route. He had to be cautious, as he had no idea if anyone was still at the site. He had even stopped to rest and remove the gag from Vivian's mouth and reload his hideout gun. He definitely wasn't aware of Oliver, who had made an end run around them and had headed the pair just as they were about to venture the last mile.

The Boss was surprised when he recognized Oliver ahead of them. He slowed both horses as they approached, but Oliver made no effort to close the gap. He just sat his horse and cautiously watched the two approach him. When the Boss and Vivian were within twenty feet, Oliver finally spoke, 'That's far enough, Boss.'

'Oliver!' the Boss said, 'What a relief. You escaped, like we did?'

'Yea, you could say that,' Oliver said, his voice even and dispassionate.

'They were killing my men!'

'Yea, they were,' Oliver said. 'I imagine they got them all.'

The Boss began to walk their horses forward and started to close the gap between them and Oliver.

Oliver just sat his horse, his left hand on the pommel of his saddle holding the reins with his right resting on his right thigh. 'I said that was far enough.'

'What? What's the matter Oliver?'

'I'm well enough,' Oliver said. 'So, Boss, why did you shoot Casper?' Oliver saw the fleeting surprise pass over the Boss' face and now he knew, just as Casper said with his dying words, the Boss had indeed killed him.

Recovering quickly, the Boss said. 'He was your enemy, what do you care?'

'He may have been my enemy, but he wasn't yours. He trusted you, and you shot him down, just like Mason.'

'Casper was trying to stop us from getting our money.'

'Our money? Don't you mean your money?'

'Now Oliver, think this through, we can still turn this around, you and me. We have the girl and that means the map, once we get to their camp. We can still ride out of here rich men!'

'Somehow I seriously doubt that,' Oliver said. 'You seem to be using up your men while your share of the pot keeps going up.'

'But you're different Oliver. You've been with me from the first, and I know your loyalty.'

'Casper was loyal. Stupid, but loyal. I saw that his gun was holstered and you still shot him. I knew you were a hard man, but killing Casper is the last straw. No one kills my kin, no one, especially with a hideout gun.'

The Boss had pulled up presenting his right side to Oliver with Vivian just behind him. Now only fifteen feet separated them. 'What is the matter with you Oliver? This is the chance we have worked for. The girl is here and we can swap her for the map. We don't have time to argue, we have to get the map and then get out of here before we are hunted down.' Then, letting both horses' reins drop, he swung his right arm out to present the desert vista before them and said, 'Once we have the map, we can go wherever we want and do what we want.'

Instantly Oliver's right hand shucked and cocked his gun and, pointing it at the Boss, shouted, 'Boss, you just stop right there!'

'You got me wrong, Oliver,' the Boss said, a steel edge to his voice while his arm was still pointing off to some distant point in the vast desert.

'Now you slowly lower that arm and let that hideout gun of yours drop on to the ground.' Oliver said slowly and gruffly. 'You even start to swing that hideout gun and I swear you'll be dead before you complete the thought.'

Seeing Oliver's pistol cocked ready to shoot and seeing the determined set of his face, the Boss slowly dropped his right hand down and the small gun slipped to the ground, landing with a heavy plop in the soft dirt. 'Very cautious of you Oliver,' the Boss said, 'but you've made a serious mistake.'

'And what mistake is that?'

'Misdirection, my friend. You were too busy watching for my hideout gun.' And as he said that, the Boss's left hand, which had been out of Oliver's sight, had been slowly drawing his left gun from its holster, and suddenly appeared around and barked. The bullet took Oliver high in the chest. In reflex Oliver's gun also went off, hitting the Boss's horse just forward of the Boss's stirrup, causing the horse to tremble. That trembling was enough to mess up the aim of the Boss's second shot, which struck Oliver higher than the Boss had aimed. Oliver's head snapped back and his hat went flying, trailed by a wisp of red.

Oliver fell back and then slid slowly to the side and off the horse, dead before he hit the ground. The Boss holstered his left gun and dismounted his trembling and bleeding mount. After picking up his hideout gun and blowing out the action, he slipped it safely up his sleeve. Then slowly walking over to Oliver, he stooped down and admired his lucky second shot. He walked over and patted Oliver's horse, as his own trembling mount collapsed. But just as he was taking the reins he heard the sound of Vivian's horse galloping in escape. He swore under his breath, 'misdirection is right,' he said aloud as he mounted Oliver's horse and rode after her.

****

The race to the stagecoach was frantic as so much depended on a timely arrival. Vivian managed to maintain her slight lead as she galloped directly into camp and was immediately challenged by the vigilant Foré: 'Stop, you!'

Seeing it was Vivian trying to dismount, Foré quickly ran forward to help her, as he could see her hands were bound. Vivian was out of breath, but between gasps she said she was being followed. No sooner were the words out of her mouth when Foré heard another horse and turned to confront this new intruder.

'No Foré, he'll kill you,' Vivian called to Foré. 'Be careful, he has a hideout gun.'

Hearing her warning, Foré drew his gun and challenged this new arrival. He was a little taken aback as the man who rode in appeared to be a gentleman, formally and immaculately dressed. But regardless of his demeanor, Foré was learning the lessons of the West and still gave his challenge: 'Stop, you mister!'

The Boss pulled up his horse and quickly dismounted, keeping his horse between Foré and himself. He walked around his horse, letting his left hand slide slowly over the horse's rump. As he did so, the Boss dropped his right arm to his side and quickly palmed his hideout gun, which slid smoothly into his hand. 'I came for the map,' he said in his aristocratic southern accent.

His pistol still trained on the man before him, Foré called over his shoulder, 'Miss Vivian, what means hideout gun?'

Before Vivian could respond, the Boss said, 'Miss Vivian, surely you do not expect this man to be your champion? I doubt he…' The Boss stopped in mid-sentence in surprise as he saw Vivian suddenly lift her dress, exposing her stockings and a pair of very shapely legs, and then slip what appeared to be an oddly shaped knife from a sheath strapped to her milky left thigh. Then, slipping the knife in her teeth, she quickly and expertly began cutting the leather bindings on her wrists. Her action so shocked the Boss that he squinted his eyes and cocked his head in disbelief. His unusual actions caused Foré also to look to his left at Vivian.

'Vivian?' Foré asked as he turned his head.

That hesitation was all the Boss needed, and using his hideout gun, he shot Foré, just as Vivian said, 'It is a gun he hides up his sleeve.'

The bullet slammed into Foré, and stumbling back, he fell to the ground in a heap, moaning softly. Then running over to Foré, the Boss kicked his gun away and turned to Vivian. He quickly pocketed his empty hideout gun and drew one of his Colts. Then with the air of confidence only arrogant breeding brings, he slowly began walking toward Vivian, his lecherous smile broadening with every step.

**\*\*\*\***

Just a hundred yards shy of their stagecoach camp, galloping side by side, Rory shouted to Lowe, 'Did you hear that?'

'Yup, smaller caliber than the last shot we heard,' Lowe shouted back, then asked, 'Vivian's?'

Rory shook his head and shouted, 'I have her purse and pistol in my saddle bag.'

Then urging his horse harder, Lowe shouted, 'The Boss is at the stagecoach!'

Seconds later with dust flying, the pair entered the camp just as the Boss was approaching Vivian. Vivian was sitting on the ground and looking like she was trying to free her wrists with something she held in her mouth. They watched in stunned silence as Vivian suddenly kicked out with her right boot, catching the Boss in the kneecap of his right leg. The man cried out, and dropping his gun, stumbled forward but barely kept himself from falling by catching the side of the stagecoach with his left hand. In a flash Vivian snapped the last of her bindings and quickly stood. Taking the knife from her mouth, she threw it, impaling the Boss's hand against the side of the stagecoach. Again the man cried out and wrenching the knife free stood up and faced Vivian, his face, recently sneering lecherously, now a mask of anger, pain and disbelief.

Lowe went to grab his right gun when Rory stopped him. 'What are you doing?' Lowe demanded.

'Hang on just a second,' Rory said. 'Shuck you gun but don't shoot. I have a theory that Vivian doesn't need our help. In fact I am beginning to wonder if she ever did.'

Both combatants were so focused on each other they were totally unaware that Rory and Lowe had ridden into the camp, and that Foré was now sitting up and watching. The Boss now cautiously limped toward Vivian. His left hand was useless, and he had dropped his Colt, but he still had the advantage of Vivian's knife. Vivian had stooped slightly, and raising both her hands, seemed totally willing to let the Boss approach, if not encouraging him by the movements of her hands.

Swinging Vivian's throwing knife left and right, slicing the air as if to punctuate his deadliness, the Boss slowly and painfully approached Vivian again, but this time more cautiously. Vivian backed up a bit, but then seemed to settle in a comfortable position and waited. When the Boss was within four feet, Vivian suddenly spun around and in a blur of motion kicked the knife from the Boss' hand. The knife flew away and landed harmlessly in the dust. Then leaping forward Vivian slammed the heel of her hand up into the Boss's nose and then 'V'-chopped the man in the throat. If that wasn't enough, she stepped back and then hopping with her left leg she kicked with her right leg square in the gut of the sorry man. The Boss had turned from an angry and deadly antagonist into a whimpering pathetic pile.

The Boss absorbed the full impact of the last kick, grunted and backed up, but did not go down. Even though his left hand was damaged, he instinctively used it to draw his left gun. The Boss tried to see through the tears and breathe through his traumatized throat while the blood slowly dripped from his broken nose. His injured hand was trying to hold his gun level as he used his right hand to pull at the collar of his shirt as if that might restore his breathing. After a gasp of air, he then turned his right hand up palm forward as if to ward off another possible frontal assault to his face and slowly took a step toward Vivian. In response, Vivian spun again only this time the kick was higher placed and it connected with the man's head, sending him to the ground on his back. In a flash Vivian leapt atop him and sent three wicked elbow strikes, one after the other into the unprotected face, splitting lips, cheeks and eyebrows. Then standing up and totally unperturbed, she looked disdainfully upon the whimpering man who had just threatened her and now lay gasping before her, cowering, torn and bleeding in his ruined suit.

Vivian looked down at her own attire, smoothed her dress down and inspected it for blood spatter. When she was satisfied, she went and retrieved her knife, and after wiping in on the Boss's pants leg, hoisted her dress and replaced the knife in its sheath. Then picking up the gun she had originally kicked from the Boss's hand, she blew out the action and spun the cylinder. Only after that did she look up to Rory and Lowe, who were sitting their horses and staring at her. Rory was amused, but Lowe was dumbfounded, his mouth hanging open. Even Foré, who was sitting up, putting pressure on a bullet wound in his thigh as Rory had taught him, stared in wonderment at the spectacle he had just witnessed, the pain from his thigh momentarily forgotten.

'I guess the cat's out of the bag,' Vivian said as she smoothed down her dress and fluffed her hair, assuming the demure façade she had used previously with these two men. Then swishing her way toward the two she said, 'I was just biding my time until I could do what I was sent here to do. I just couldn't help myself,' she said, indicating the man she had just demolished. 'I have wanted to do that to him from the time they kidnapped me.'

'Who are you?' asked Lowe, still stupefied by the athletic and brutal demonstration he had just witnessed.

Before Vivian could answer Lowe, Rory said, 'I would say we just witnessed an excellent demonstration of mixed martial arts.' Then turning to Lowe, he said, 'I think the question we should be asking is not *who* she is, but *what* is she?'

'What do you mean Rory?' Lowe asked.

'He is suggesting, Mr Lowe, that I am not just a young woman off to meet up with her guardian,' Vivian said, continuing to walk over to the two men, who still sat their horses.

'What she is?' said Lowe, his face still a jumble of questions. 'What do you mean?'

'I have seen only a few individuals who could use a throwing knife so efficiently, and even fewer who fight like that,' Rory said. 'Training like that takes time and practice.'

'I still don't understand,' Lowe said, looking from Rory to Vivian and back again.

'What I want to know is, why you didn't just kill him with the knife?' Rory asked. 'Why did you feel the need to beat him?'

'I had suffered too much at the hands of that vicious man not to derive some satisfaction. Justice was required here. Justice for him and for me.' Vivian said. 'He deserves to die, but I will leave that up to you two.'

Then turning to Foré, Vivian called over, 'Are you going to be okay Mr Foré?'

'Y...Yes, Miss Vivian,' Foré said. 'I again am shot. Is not serious. I am put pressure and wait for Rory to help as before.'

Turning back to Rory and Lowe, Vivian calmly asked, 'Do either of you have my purse?'

'It is in my saddle bag,' Rory said.

'I am pleased,' Vivian said. 'I didn't want to return to that camp to retrieve it. Would you please get it for me?'

Turning in his saddle, Rory slipped the thong on his saddle bag, and as he pulled out Vivian's purse said, 'I don't not know if it still has all your belongings.'

'Does it have my gun?'

'Yes, but not your handkerchief.'

'Oh, you can keep the handkerchief as a souvenir, but that gun was a gift from President Jefferson Davis himself,' she said. 'Would you please toss my purse over to me?'

'President Jefferson Davis?' Lowe asked incredulously.

'Yes. I have been in his employ for the last couple of years. I was assigned to protect what I believe you are carrying, Mr Lowe. I'm sorry for my deception, but I thought it would make things easier if I appeared to be a naive and helpless young woman inexperienced in the ways of the world and in need of protection.'

As comprehension dawned on Lowe, he angrily asked, 'Protect what I am carrying? Are you telling me we just risked our lives to save you, and it was all for nothin? All for that stupid map?'

'It was not for nothing, Mr Lowe. You were very gallant and I appreciate your chivalry.'

154

'Chivalry?' Lowe asked.

'She is referring to the moral system of medieval knights who protected the weak,' Rory said.

'Well, thanks for that, but we thought you were in real danger. You could have escaped all along and we wouldn't have had to come to your rescue and get shot in the process!' Lowe said, the anger in his voice showing. 'So you are what? Some sort of spy for the Confederacy?'

'I prefer the term undercover agent of the Confederacy,' Vivian said. 'I am truly sorry for getting you shot. None of this was part of the plan. I was just along to make sure you delivered the map as agreed. My superior believed information about the map may have gotten out, as an important contact came up missing, and so I was sent to ensure all went well.'

'All for nothing. Just some stupid map,' Lowe said, his anger now stoked with frustration and regret. 'I wish I had never accepted this job.'

'Well, I'm sorry for your injuries, but at least I can save you the trouble of delivering the map. So, if you will give me the map, I will leave you,' Vivian said.

Lowe looked at Vivian in amazement. After all they had done. She was just going to take the map and ride off. Rory could see Lowe's methodical mind working through it all, and he wasn't sure just what Lowe was going to do.

'No, I took the job and I will see it through,' Lowe finally said.

'Chivalrous to the end, Mr Lowe, but I insist,' Vivian said as she lifted the gun she had retrieved from the Boss and pointed it at Lowe.

Rory could see Lowe weighing his options, and before he could act, said, 'Lowe, let me see the map,' Rory stated in his reassuring leader's tone. After a short hesitation by Lowe, Rory prompted, 'Come on Lowe, hand it over.'

Lowe looked at Rory, then at Vivian, and finally at Rory again. Then nodding slowly, he pulled the packet from his boot and handed it to Rory. Rory took the small package, unwrapped the oilskin and again inspected the map, but this time with greater scrutiny. He held it up to the light and nodded. He then wrapped it up again and tossed it to Vivian, who deftly caught it in her left hand and then stuffed it into her purse.

'Now if you gentlemen will drop your guns, I will leave you,' Vivian said. 'You need to drop your gun as well, Mr Foré,' she said over her shoulder. 'And Rory, you will need to drop the hideout gun in your boot.'

'I can't believe I told you about that,' Rory said as he shot Lowe an embarrassed glance and saw Lowe was looked at him in disgust. 'You sure fooled me.'

After making sure they dropped all their weapons, Vivian went over to the stagecoach and took some of the remaining food and a canteen. Then swinging into the saddle, she walked her horse back over to Rory, and keeping her gun drawn, she leaned over and kissed him on the cheek. 'Believe it or not but I will miss you Rory,' she said, giving him the dazzling smile that had smitten him earlier.

Rory turned a bright red and Lowe just grunted in disgust.

Then turning to Lowe, Vivian said, 'Your job is done here, Mr Lowe, so let's leave it at that, shall we? I will report that you did your job. You actually went beyond expectations and you definitely earned your money.'

Even though Vivian had him covered, Lowe started forward, but Rory reached out and grabbed his horse's reins.

'Let her go, Lowe,' Rory said. 'She has the drop on us and I believe she would make good on her threat.'

'Very wise, Rory. I don't want to hurt either of you,' Vivian said. 'I have what I came for, and though I appreciate your actions on my behalf, I assure you, Mr Lowe, I have everything in control.'

'Just don't cross my path in the future, Vivian. I don't forget injuries. Blood spilt in friendship should be sacred, but you might as well have shot me yourself,' Lowe said. And with that, as if planned, the two men turned their horses and walked over to check on Foré.

Vivian looked at the two departing men, shrugged and encouraged her horse into a steady lope in the direction of the next weigh-station. 'I'll encourage the hostlers to come get you when I see them,' Vivian called back, 'and be sure they collect and store my luggage.' Soon she was just a speck of dust in the vast plain.

When they reached Foré, Rory dismounted and even though Lowe protested, Rory helped him down from his saddle. While Rory started treating Foré's wound, Lowe returned and gathered up the weapons Vivian had ordered them to throw down. Picking up each with his right hand, he blew them off before slipping them behind his belt. He then went to the Boss and collected his guns too, including the little hideout gun. Then returning to the other two, he gave them back. 'They'll need cleaning,' he cautioned.

'Just set mine aside for now, Lowe,' Rory said. 'And thanks.'

'Here Foré, you can have the Boss's hideout gun. It's just a one-shot derringer, but it's a good gun to have,' Lowe said.

'Thank you, Mr Lowe,' said Foré. 'You will teach me to use?'

'Sure. I may be crippled, but I pull my weight.'
'And no one would suggest otherwise,' Rory said reassuringly. 'You've done you share, and more.'

'Thanks Rory, that means a lot to me. So, what are we going to do with the Boss? Vivian near beat him to death. I thought that last kick to the head would have killed him.'

'It very well could have,' Rory responded while checking on Foré. After additional inspection he said, 'Foré, you are one lucky Frenchman! You get shot twice and both times they are simple flesh wounds.'

'And I ready to go,' Foré interjected. 'I am fun to write back home about this. I am shot two times in American West!'

'I had my doubts about you, Foré,' Lowe stated, 'but I would trust you to watch my back any day!'

'What means "watch back"?' Foré asked Rory, who was finishing up treating the wound.

'Lowe just paid you one of the greatest compliments. He meant he would trust you with his safety in a fight.'

'Thank you my friend,' Foré said to Lowe. Lowe nodded and went back to cleaning his guns, somewhat embarrassed by Foré's show of affection. Rory saw the interchange, and was more and more convinced that Lowe wanted acceptance, but his hard exterior, built layer by layer throughout his life, made it difficult for him to believe in others.

'So what is the plan?' Lowe asked, inclining his head over to the Boss.

'Is he still alive?' Rory asked.

'He's still breathing, if that's what you mean, but I doubt he is alive. I mean, what man could face getting the tar beat out of him by a bound woman?' Lowe said.

'Well, in all fairness, she wasn't just a woman and she wasn't bound when she did the most damage,' Rory said.

'Yes, I see her happy kicks,' Foré said. 'But she also carry weapons in special places,' he said with a grin.

'Just think of the stories you can tell when you set up your winery!' Rory laughed. 'You are fitting right in.'

After ensuring Foré was patched up, Rory threaded a needle with a horse's tail hair and prepared to stitch up Lowe's exit wound once it was sterilized with the last of Foré's liquor.

Foré actually offered Rory the last of his flask as they prepared to stitch up Lowe's side, with the lament, 'Oh, waste of grape – but is good to you, Mr Lowe!'

It took a few minutes with Lowe grunting in pain after each stitch. When Rory had finished he stood up and said, 'Okay, as I see it we have two options. We can either wait here until we are rescued by the stage line, or we can ride out,' Rory said.

'We have only two horses with... What is the word for horse clothes?' Foré asked.

'Saddles?' ventured Lowe.

'Yes, and I don't know if I can ride to station without saddle,' Foré said apologetically.

'And what about the Boss?' Lowe said, pointing to the crumpled unconscious man.

Rory looked at the Boss, and said, 'I think we should go to the other camp, bury the dead, recover any supplies, then return here and wait for the stage line. They should arrive sometime today. When they get here they can take care of him.'

Then turning to Rory, Lowe asked, 'And Vivian?'

'Let her go. We may yet meet up with her in the future.'

'Why do you say that?' Lowe asked.

'Because I know she will have a lot of explaining to do to her superiors.'

'Why is that?'

'Well, the map you gave her is a fake. When I looked it over more carefully, I recognized it as one of Pegleg's bogus maps. He made several and sold them to unsuspecting miners when I was in California.'

'You've been to California?' Foré asked.

'You do get around,' Lowe commented.

'Being a newspaper reporter requires sacrifice,' Rory said grinning. 'So, as the map is fake, I figure the Confederacy will either give up on that money-making scheme, or they will think you gave Vivian a decoy. And if they believe you kept the real map, they will come after you. Maybe they will even send Vivian.'

'Well, there is justice after all,' said Lowe. 'My only regret is that I couldn't be there to see the look on Vivian's face.'

'Amen, brother. Amen!'